THE BARBED WIRE NOOSE

Carl Wilcox found Foote—swaying and twisting ever so gently, from a barbed wire noose. As a blizzard envelops the town, Foote's survivors and other interested parties gather at the Corden Hotel: Kitty and Buff, Foote's children; Johnstone, Kitty's big-city sugar daddy, and his torpedo O'Keefe; Gregory Plante, the fatuous son of a radio evangelist. Not least, there's the ghost of Azalea Foote, a secretive woman who died with her unnamed baby in a fire ten years earlier. As Wilcox tears through the fabric of deceit, the horrors of the past invade the hotel. One of the guests is dead—naked in the sub-zero temperatures outside. And everyone has an alibi.

THE BARBED WIRE NOOSE

Harold Adams

ATLANTIC LARGE PRINT
Chivers Press, Bath, England.
Curley Publishing, Inc.,
South Yarmouth, Mass., USA.

ADA LARGE PRINT

Library of Congress Cataloging-in-Publication Data

Adams, Harold, 1923–
    The barbed wire noose / Harold Adams.
        p.   cm.—(Atlantic large print)
    "An Atlantic book"—Jacket.
    ISBN 0–7927–0073–2 (lg. print)
    1. Large type books.   I. Title.
[PS3551.D367B3   1990]
813'.54—dc20   89–23424
                                                                          CIP

British Library Cataloguing in Publication Data

Adams, Harold, 1923–
    The barbed wire noose.
    I. Title
    823'.914 [F]

    ISBN 0–7451–9666–7
    ISBN 0–7451–9677–2 pbk

This Large Print edition is published by Chivers Press, England, and
Curley Publishing, Inc, U.S.A. 1990

Published in the British Commonwealth by arrangement with the author
and in the U.S.A. with Warner Books, Inc

U.K. Hardback ISBN 0 7451 9666 7
U.K. Softback ISBN 0 7451 9677 2
U.S.A. Softback ISBN 0 7927 0073 2

To Gail Myers,
lifelong friend, who knew
Corden better than I.

THE BARBED WIRE NOOSE

CHAPTER ONE

The cold wind moaned and the shack creaked. I stared at the body, swaying and twisting ever so gently from a barbed wire noose. There was no smell even though I could see dark stains down the frozen pants. The neck was stretched and blood had frozen soon after oozing from barbs that had penetrated flesh under the once flabby chin.

'Well, Foote,' I said, 'you always had to do things the hard way, right?'

He didn't answer.

I looked for something to stand on so I could let him down but there wasn't a box, stool or chair in sight, only snow in small drifts built through cracks in the walls. It dawned on me that Foote hadn't got himself into this fix without help.

'Well, shit,' I thought and clumped back outside where the free wind slashed my face with icy snow.

*   *   *

Joey was slumped at his desk in City Hall, drinking coffee with one hand and tucking an old shawl around his neck with the other. An electric heater, glowing red, sat on the floor pointed at his knees.

1

'Help yourself,' he said, tilting his head toward the coffeepot on the hot plate. 'Was it Foote?'

I poured coffee and nodded.

'Somebody hung him up. With barbed wire.'

He lowered his cup and let his chin sag. 'My God. You sure it wasn't suicide?'

'Not unless somebody strolled in and swiped whatever he stood on to do the job. I couldn't find a thing to climb on so I could let him down.'

'You'd best borrow a stepladder from Elihu and do that. It ain't right to leave him hanging.'

'I don't think he'll notice. There's nothing there now but frozen meat.'

'It was a man,' he said reproachfully.

'It isn't now.'

Joey wasn't ever much good at philosophy, he was all stuck on propriety. I gave him a little more trouble before getting the ladder and recruiting Ernie Deckert to haul the body down to Doc Feeney's office for an autopsy. I was glad the carcass was frozen because even without any stink, Ernie almost got sick when he piped Foote's stretched neck and the other little details.

Doc Feeney wasn't the least bit thrilled by our present. He said there was no way he could handle a body like that and insisted we take it to Aquatown. Ernie refused to make

2

the delivery until I agreed to ride along and protect him in case Foote thawed out and turned mean along the way.

People at the hospital morgue accepted our package as if things like that arrived every afternoon and afterward I offered to buy Ernie a cup of coffee before we headed back. After one cup he perked up enough to order a slab of apple pie, which he ate with an appetite that seemed pretty disrespectful to me, but I couldn't shame him.

'Who you figure'd want to murder old Foote?' he asked me while he was slurping his second cup.

'Probably a jealous husband.'

He scoffed. 'That scruffy old bastard? What woman'd be interested in him?'

'A motherly type. The ones that bring around soup for lonely old widowers.'

'Naw. More likely some mean kids done it. The ones he was always chasing off the lot 'cause they were swiping gooseberries and wild plums. He figured they was his.'

'He owned the lot?'

'I suppose. He owned the house that was on it once. It burned down, let's see ... over ten years ago ... more'n that ... I hear it was almost paid for and then it was gone and he didn't have no insurance. He kept drifting back there, like an ol' ghost. He did have a woman, once.'

'A wife?'

3

'Uh-huh. And three kids: boy, girl and a baby. Boy run off and joined the navy. The wife died with the baby in the fire. Girl went off to Aquatown I think. Lived with an aunt till she finished high school.'

'The aunt?'

'Naw, the girl. Name was Kitty. Kitty Foote. Kids used to call her Pussyfoot. She didn't like it.'

I sat back, marveling. If Ernie and my old man, Elihu, got together they could write a history of Corden that'd run longer than *The Fall of the Roman Empire*. Nobody could fart without their recording it in their thick heads and then sitting around itching for a chance to spout it all.

'How'd this Kitty do in school?' I asked.

'Just fine. Had some spats with kids, because of the nickname, you know. She whipped a boy once. In a fair fight. Well, it was pretty fair, she got hold of his hair and just banged him around till he about died. Nobody in reach called her Pussyfoot much after that. At least not any that weren't a lot bigger. There's a story she crocked one sixth grader with a rock the size of your fist. She was a third grader at the time. I ain't sure that story's true—never talked to anybody saw her do it.'

I liked that. It was good to know he looked for verification of all the tales he told.

'How'd the sailor do?'

'In school? He didn't fight much. Sort of one of them sly kind that nobody notices, you know?'

'Anybody hear from him after he joined up?'

'Not as I know of. Never came back.'

'Well, it seems to me that considering your stock of knowledge, you'd be the most likely fella to tell me who'd do in old Foote the way it was done.'

'No notion,' he said. 'How about we have another cup?'

It was starting to snow when we pulled onto the highway and before long we couldn't see a car a block ahead. Old Ernie bent over the wheel and kept urging the wipers on, but they didn't put themselves out any, and the windshield was streaked and snow-spotted so bad we slowed to a crawl. We could've made better time walking but didn't consider it because the wind was blowing enough to pull the socks out of your boots.

Pretty soon Ernie was watching telephone poles to tell where the highway went. That worked until we got past Jimtown and then he forgot the poles, took a shortcut at Bentley's curve and the next thing we were plowing through a ditch and got hung up on the fence bordering a pasture. The snow wasn't real deep yet, so Ernie was able to rock us out, and after a lot of swearing, shifting and wheel spinning he got us back on the

5

road.

I asked him if he knew anybody who'd been a friend to Foote and he said no, he'd never seen him even talking to anybody except Boswell.

'Even a lizard'll talk to Boswell,' he said as he hunched forward, trying to see the road.

We only got off once more before finally easing into the shallow valley bordering the eastern edge of Corden and a few minutes later we were parked in front of City Hall.

We found Joey inside, asleep with his head in his arms on the desk. I woke him and he raised a red, sweating face.

'You got a fever,' I said.

'A little,' he admitted.

'I'm gonna call Doc.'

He didn't argue and I knew he was sick.

Two hours later he was home in bed. An hour after that Mayor Syvertson came around to find me in the Wilcox Hotel lobby, smoking a cigarette and chinning with Elihu, who was sitting in his swivel chair watching the snowstorm with the deep satisfaction of a man warm and fed, who had hired help that'd shovel the place out.

The mayor greeted Elihu with all the respect due a man who'd voted for him regular and sat down across from me after hitching up his crease to keep it from cracking from the pressure of his fat knees.

'We got a little problem,' he said.

6

'Snowplow busted?' I asked.

'Not that I know of. What we got is no town cop. Doc tells me Joey's got pneumonia.'

I said I was sorry to hear that and meant it.

He agreed in a tone that suggested it might be the greatest tragedy since Lincoln's assassination. Then he squirmed some, like a third grader in a schoolchair, and said that since I'd been a good friend of Joey's and had worked with him some in the past and knew how to handle drunks and wasn't doing much of anything constructive or profitable, how'd I like to sort of temporarily take the job till Joey was well?

I told him the notion was about as inviting as the idea of taking a naked stroll down Main in our current blizzard.

'You'd get almost the same pay as Joey,' he said. 'Not the same, of course, since you haven't had his experience, but pretty close.'

That'd be more money than I'd ever made on an hourly basis except for the time I took on the carnival pro in a boxing sideshow.

I shook my head.

He leaned back in the brown rocker and nodded.

'Okay. I had to ask 'cause Joey suggested it. He was probably feverish anyway. If you took the job I'd have half the town screaming at me. Can't you just imagine the talk if I hired a man who'd been in prison twice?'

7

Elihu snorted. 'I'd be one of 'em talking.'

I knew I was being had but could no more control my reaction than a cat dropped from a window.

'When you want me to start?'

'Right now,' said Syvertson as he got up. 'Puck Olson's drunk over at Bond's Cafe and kicking up a rumpus. Come on.'

I went into the hall for my shortcoat, came back, exchanged looks with my old man and for just a second caught the gleam in his fox eyes before he returned his attention to the falling snow outside.

Puck was past his prime but still as mean and ready as when he'd played hockey for the University of Minnesota over a dozen years before. He'd worked on construction crews, mixing cement, pushing barrows and swinging shovels after he flunked out of school. Then work disappeared and for the last couple of years he'd mostly done odd jobs when he could scrape them up.

We found him sitting at the far end of the counter. At first glance everything looked very peaceful. There were about half a dozen customers scattered among the booths along the east wall and a few others at the tables. Bond was standing behind the counter, his cook, Billy, was standing in the kitchen door and just behind I could see Rose's dark head.

I looked back at Puck and saw he was holding Bond's sawed-off pool cue in his right

8

fist. That was a little persuader Bond kept handy beside the cash register in case anyone got too starchy.

'There he is,' said Syvertson. 'Talk to him.'

'I see him,' I said. 'The only trouble is, you didn't give me any of the tools of my job yet.'

'He'll listen to you. Go on.'

I walked toward the back and took a stool one removed from Puck.

He looked at me and waggled the cue gently.

'How's it going, Puck?' I asked.

'Horseshit,' he said profoundly.

'That's the usual way. How come you got Bond's pool cue?'

He grinned. 'Just borrowing it. Thought I might want to play a game.'

'I think it's a little short to work very well.'

He scowled past me at the mayor. 'It'll reach any ball I want to hit.'

I put both elbows on the counter.

'You sore at somebody?'

'I just ain't gonna take no shit.'

'Somebody trying to hand you some?'

'Uh-huh.' He nodded toward the mayor. '*That* asshole.'

I glanced back at Syvertson, who bravely held his place handy to the door.

'You need a pool cue to handle the mayor?'

'This here's for Joey when he shows.'

'You try to use that stick on Joey and he'll show you why he carries a gun.'

9

Puck shook his head. 'Joey ain't ever shot nobody. He just clubs 'em. A pool cue's a better club than a gun any day.'

'Why you want to fight Joey?'

'He works for that asshole, that's why.'

I took my elbows off the counter, faced him square and moved to the stool next to him.

'I got bad news for you, friend. Tonight I'm working for him because Joey's sick. You want to put that cue down and go home?'

His mouth sagged.

'You're the law in Corden?'

I grinned. 'How about that?'

He stared for a few seconds, then began laughing. I joined him. When I started to lower my head he brought the cue around in a tight arc that ended when his wrist hit my left fist and I hooked him in the gut. His stool went over backward, landing him on the floor with a bang so hard his head bounced off the boards and suddenly he was peaceful as a sleeping doll.

Bond brought me Puck's coat and when he was able to navigate I helped him to his feet and walked him out into the deepening snow.

'I shoulda seen you were sober,' Puck told me sorrowfully. 'I shoulda known something was horseshit. Why tha' hell'd you club me?'

'You bounced your noggin on the floor when I nudged you off the stool,' I told him. 'Why'd you want in jail again?'

10

He said because it'd be warm and don't bother taking him to his room because he'd been locked out. He didn't have anyplace to sleep. So I took him to the jail and left him sleeping quietly. I appreciated the fact that he hadn't asked how come I'd sold out. I didn't think I had, much. I was just helping out Joey and spiting my old man.

CHAPTER TWO

No parade of citizens came around the next morning to congratulate me for becoming the town cop. That didn't hurt my feelings, but I was some put out that nobody I heard of made a stink about the appointment.

Mayor Syvertson came around to tell me how I was supposed to patrol downtown after closing time and check to see if merchants had locked their doors. I was also told to drop in on the pool hall and visit the beer parlor, which had opened since the end of Prohibition, but I was absolutely not allowed to touch beer or spirits. I asked was it okay to smoke and speak to girls and he said of course but it would be nice if I'd buy ready-made cigarettes and I said fine, if they'd be included in my expenses and after a short conference we compromised and I kept rolling my own.

11

The one good thing about politicians is the wise ones know when to compromise. The dumb ones don't know anything else.

Boswell was my first visitor. I was flattered because when there's fresh snow that old man stays in his cabin by the railroad tracks until enough people wander by to pack it down and make the walking easy. On this particular morning we had six inches of the stuff under a blank, blue sky and a cold, pale sun made the world so bright everybody's face hurt from squinching up their eyes against the ungodly glare. It was twenty-one below with no wind.

On days like that you can walk outside bareheaded and think it's all very lovely until after a block your ears fall off.

I was sitting in Joey's office at City Hall, drinking coffee and shooting the breeze with Puck when Boswell showed up. He was wearing his black stocking cap with a scarf wrapped around it, another scarf around his neck and chin, and boots so big I couldn't believe he had the strength to lift them, let alone walk. It took about ten minutes for him to get unwrapped and find his hands under his huge mitts.

He didn't ask how come I was the town cop or how it felt to jail a man for disorderly conduct and that was fine, but even better I didn't feel any need to explain.

I asked him was it cold out and he said just

12

brisk.

'You heard about Foote?' I asked.

'Hung himself.'

'You think that's likely? I mean, that he'd do it with barbed wire?'

'Oh, yah.'

'There was nothing else in the shack to use,' said Puck.

I looked at him. His eyes were so bloodshot it was a wonder they didn't flow red. He needed a shave. Boswell did too but his eyes were clear and gentle as a mother's with a baby at her breast.

'You ever talk with Foote?' I asked Boswell.

He nodded.

'He talk with anybody else—have any friends you know of?'

He shook his head, tamped down his pipe with his middle finger, lit a wooden match and began puffing. Thick white smoke floated up and around his hairy ears.

'He didn't grow up here, where'd he come from?'

'Aberdeen, I think.'

'He marry there?'

'Yup. Little Norsky gal. They come here while she was big with her first.'

'It never come from Foote,' said Puck.

'How'd you know?'

'Hell, you only had to look at the son of a bitch to know that. What kinda woman'd let

13

him stick it in her?'

'The kind that'd marry him.' I turned back to Boswell. 'What'd Foote do in Aberdeen?'

'Worked in a jewelry store. Watchmaker.'

'What'd he do here?'

'Worked for Arhart a spell. When Arhart let him go, he didn't do much of nothing. Kept a garden till his wife died.'

'What'd he do for money?'

Boswell shrugged.

'Did the wife work?'

'Not for money.'

I remembered that when Joey and I went through his pockets, Foote had twelve dollars in his wallet and fifty-seven cents in his purse. There wasn't much of anything else but two paper clips, a dull pen knife with a cracked mother of pearl handle and a hard piece of chewing gum still in its wrapper. Spearmint.

'He had to be getting money somewhere,' I said.

Boswell shrugged and disappeared in a cloud as he restoked his pipe.

We were still sitting there, thinking, when the mayor showed up. His cheeks were ruddy with cold and they didn't lose any color when he saw Puck sitting in Joey's office with a sociable cup of coffee cradled in his horny hands.

I was asked in official tones what the prisoner was doing out of his cell and I said from all appearances he was having a cup of

14

coffee.

Syvertson advised me that prisoners were to be confined to their cells and was going into the details when Puck, with a look of disgust, got up. Syvertson quickly backed out of his way and watched as he went through the fire engine room and on back to the cell, which he entered and slammed the door behind him with a clang. Then he flopped on the bunk and closed his eyes.

'Well,' said the mayor, 'you appear to have things under control, but really, Carl, you can't be this casual.'

'I was interrogating him,' I said with a straight face.

His eyebrows about disappeared under his hat brim.

'What about?'

'The Foote murder.'

He looked back toward the cell. 'You think he did it?'

'Nope. You know what Foote lived on?'

He thought about that and finally shook his head. 'No, I remember wondering about it a time or two. It's worth looking into, isn't it?'

'I thought so.'

'Still, it'd be a lot simpler if we just concluded it was a suicide, wouldn't it?'

I agreed it would.

We talked a little about how I should keep the report record up-to-date and make arrangements for Judge Wilkerson to see

Puck in the afternoon.

'Oh,' I said, 'does the judge need some wood split?'

'I'm sure he'll find some useful task for Puck to perform,' he said with a prim look. Then, pausing at the door, he advised me not to have personal friends visiting too much in the office and left.

Boswell stuck around long enough to fumigate the City Hall with his stinking pipe and drink three cups of coffee before drifting off on his own rounds. I put on my jacket and waded east to the hotel.

Elihu was down in the main cellar, feeding the coal furnace when I found him and wanted to know when I was going to shovel the walk. I told him it was beneath the dignity of the town cop and he swore awhile but didn't really have his heart in it.

'Listen,' I said, 'you do me a favor, I'll do you one, okay?'

He put the shovel down and glowered at me through his bushy white eyebrows.

'Like what?'

'You know what Foote lived on?'

'You gonna shovel the walk?'

'Why not?'

'He got a check the first of every month.'

'How'd you know that?'

'I know R. J. Swenson, the postman, that's how. You gonna do the walk now?'

'How much was the check for?'

16

'R.J. just delivers the mail, he don't read it.'

'I bet he candles it.'

'If he does, he don't tell me what he sees.'

'When'd his wife die?'

'R.J.'s never been married. Too short.'

'I meant Foote's wife.'

'Five years or so.'

'What from?'

Elihu peered into the furnace, which glared back, reddening his cheeks and tinting his silver hair pink. He slammed the iron door shut, hung the shovel on a wall peg and started past me toward the stairs.

'Died in their house. With her baby.'

'When did the older girl leave?'

'A little after.'

'The girl leave mad?'

'Nope. Needed work, couldn't find it here. Went to Aquatown, then to the cities. Why don't you get that walk cleared?'

It was mostly fluff, so I got the job done in jig time but still wasn't quick enough to finish before Syvertson came by to ask what I thought I was doing.

'Keeping the peace,' I said.

'How so?'

'If I don't shovel this walk my old man will be screeching bloody murder. Do you know any way we can find out where Foote got a check from every month?'

He thought awhile and said no, not unless

17

R. J. Swenson remembered.

So when R.J. came around I asked him.

I'm not tall, so you can get some notion of R.J.'s stature when I tell you with him standing and me sitting we were near equal eye level. He had the build of a beer keg and the face of a dissipated cherub. For several seconds after I asked my question he stood beside Joey's desk, pinning me with his brown stare.

'Come on, R.J.,' I said, 'I'm not asking you how much the check was for or who signed it, just where it came from. They got a return address on the envelope, don't they?'

'I was thinking,' he said.

'Yeah, I can see the smoke, so what do you remember?'

'I think it was a bank in Aberdeen. I looked at the address the first few times when it came, but after a while I didn't pay it any mind. It was always the same, I think.'

'He get any other mail?'

'Uh-huh. About a month ago, mebbe more. When we got that wet snow—'

'Where'd it come from?'

'Right here in Corden.'

'Yeah? Who sent it?'

'It didn't have no return on it. I looked on both sides.'

'Was the address printed or written?'

'Hand-printed. Big letters. It had on it "Dirty Foote. Corden, South Dakota."

18

That's all. I knew who it was meant for.'

'That the only mail he got?'

'Oh, he heard from Kitty now and again. That was his daughter, you know. He never got nothing from the boy. Buff. For Buford.'

After lunch I moseyed over to Abigail Brown's little white house and knocked. She opened the inside door and spoke to me through the storm.

'What do *you* want?'

'I'd like to talk with you about old Foote.'

'I ain't talkin' to you, I don't care what that fool Syvertson has done, making you the lawman.'

'Look, Abigail, I'm not real excited about talking with you either, but neither of us got much choice. Foote's dead. I got to see his things and try to find out where his son and daughter might be so I can let them know.'

'I'll give you their addresses. Wait here.'

She didn't give me a chance to remind her it was ten below out; she just closed the inner door and went away. I stomped my feet, rolled a smoke and glared across the street at Mrs. Sorenson, who was staring out her front window at me. She ducked back out of sight.

A while later Abigail was back. She opened the storm a crack and slipped an old envelope through. I took it, looked over the two addresses and started to thank her, but she got the door slammed shut and was gone before I got my mouth open.

19

I was working on a letter to the offspring when I got a telephone call from an eager young doctor at the hospital in Aquatown. He said Foote had died from strangulation, but before that he'd been beaten so bad he had a ruptured spleen, two cracked ribs and a skull fracture. He'd also been pounded in the groin area. He said that after all that, there was no way Foote could have managed to stand up, let alone hang himself.

He promised to have a written report to me by morning. I thanked him, hung up and sat for a long time thinking about the poor bastard. I wondered what he'd looked like when he was young and if he got any satisfaction out of working on watches or being married to a Norsky girl and fathering three kids. I tried to remember what he'd looked like alive, but all that came to mind was what I'd found in the shack.

After a while I decided the hell with writing letters and called the telephone operator to get numbers for the offspring. It turned out the son was at sea on a destroyer off the Pacific coast. I was told they'd radio the news to him. The officer I talked with was pretty impatient when I couldn't tell him the date of the funeral.

I called Scanlon's funeral parlor and learned from Sid that it'd be on Friday, which was three days away.

Then I called Minneapolis and got Kitty's

20

number. I didn't really expect to make the connection, but after three rings a husky voice said, 'Yes?'

I asked for Kitty Foote.

'You got her.'

'Oh—you got a cold, huh?'

'You're psychic,' she said. 'Can you do readings?'

'I don't know, never tried. Listen, this is Carl Wilcox, in Corden—'

'Old Wild Wilcox? The fighting man?'

'I'm not old and haven't had a fight for two days. As a matter of fact, I'm sitting in for the town cop, Joey—'

'You're kidding. Carl Wilcox, the convict, is Corden's cop?'

'Kitty, this call's no joke. I got news about your dad.'

There was a second's pause.

'What's happened?'

'I'm sorry, but he's dead.'

'Ah.'

She coughed, once, then several times, muttered something about wait and I could hear the phone receiver being set on a hard surface. A few seconds later she was back.

'Had to get some water. So, what'd he die of?'

'It was murder.'

There was a long silence.

'The funeral's gonna be Friday.'

After another long silence I asked if she

21

was going to come and she said, yeah, if she didn't die of pneumonia first. She didn't say goodbye, just hung up.

The mayor agreed to come along with me to Abigail Smith's, where he soon persuaded her that his company would protect her from ravishment and robbery, so we got in and examined the room that had been Foote's only home for the past five years.

It was a little bigger than mine at the hotel and considerably more cluttered. He hardly had more than two full changes of clothing for street wear and there were four suits of summer BVD's and two pairs of long johns, all with fart blossom stains in the seat. He must've had a serious problem because Abigail did his laundry and was famous for her work with strong soap and lots of bleach. His five pair of spare shoes had run-down heels and soles so thin he'd put cardboard inside. There was no mirror in the room.

He'd saved no envelopes from the Aberdeen bank, but I found a small packet of letters from Kitty in the top left drawer of the bureau. The right top drawer was stacked with *Spicy Westerns, Spicy Mysterys* and *Spicy Romances*, plus a few assorted horror pulps. They all sported covers with ladies in unlikely get-ups that showed all the skin the law'd allow and maybe a bit more. All the women were either screaming or swooning.

In with the socks I found the letter R.J.

had delivered on the wet-snow day.

Dirty Foote. You son of a bitch, you're going to get yours! Think about it, you goddamned pervert. THINK ABOUT IT!!!!!!

I showed it to the mayor, who sighed and shook his head.
'Why'd a man save a thing like that?'
I didn't know.
In the bottom drawer, under the long johns, I found two bank books, one savings, one checking. I saw he'd been depositing forty dollars a month in savings and twenty in the checking account. In December he'd written a check for twenty-five dollars, but it didn't say who it was to. I flipped back a ways and saw the December before he'd written one for fifteen and another for ten, but, again, it didn't say who they were for. I guess when you only write one or two checks a year it isn't too tough a job figuring out who they were for.
We walked from Abigail's over to the bank, where James J. Bangston, the president, gave us his thousand-dollar smile and not one cent's worth of help. So we went to Judge Wilkerson for a court order and returned to the bank for Foote's records. J.J. gave us a thoughtful frown, weighed the danger of arousing the wrath of a deceased customer

23

against the risks of crossing the judge and promptly turned cooperative as a stool pigeon in a jail basement.

The checks came from a trust fund in an Aberdeen bank. They were for one hundred dollars.

After some debate with the mayor I was allowed to call the Aberdeen bank. Its president was delighted to be of service. All he wanted was a copy of the death certificate before he'd tell us anything. I was all for getting another court order, but the mayor said that'd be a little more complicated since he didn't know any judges in that town. He said there was no big hurry, we'd just mail the certificate and follow up in time.

I figured, what the hell, by then maybe Joey'd be well and none of this would be any of my business.

When we had gone to see the judge we took Puck along and the judge gave him a suspended sentence, so he was on his own. Puck asked if I thought Abigail would let him take Foote's room since Foote'd paid in advance and there was still two weeks in the month and nobody else was using the space.

I told him he had all the chance of a mosquito in a sleet storm, but he decided to try anyway. Not too many things surprise me in Corden, but Abigail about floored me when she let the man in. I didn't find out until two months later that he'd worked her by saying

24

I'd told him she wouldn't dare let him past the doorsill.

She'd rather get raped than have me right about anything.

CHAPTER THREE

Elihu had his first stroke that evening. He was sitting at the dining room table, shoveling in mashed potatoes, when all of a sudden he dropped the fork, looked at me with a shocked expression, slouched back and slid under the table. I got him stetched out and loosened his collar while Ma ran for the telephone and called Doc. He came running and before long had the old man in his bed. Pretty soon Elihu began coming around, but his tongue was thick and his eyes glazed.

Doc said we'd ought to get him to the hospital in Aquatown. Ma vetoed that. She said he'd be better off in his own bed, he'd been to the hospital once and they'd blamed near killed him.

Doc asked me if I could talk sense into her and I said no. We talked it over awhile out in the lobby and he finally allowed as how Ma might be right. We'd see how the old man was in the morning and go from there.

It was near nine when I started on my rounds. Every store was tight-locked and snug. It was a clear night, twenty-five below and little wind. The snow creaked under my boots and my breath was a small cloud moving before me, drifting up to dampen my cheeks, which I kept wiping dry with my mitts. I stopped in at the beer parlor with its pool hall in the back and Gus, the bartender, asked about Elihu. I said he seemed to be sleeping okay. Most of the loungers were too young to know or care about the old man, they were interested in giving me a hard time. They wanted to know where my gun was and one smartass said I carried my billy between my legs. Nobody asked to see my badge. It was inside my shirt pocket. Mayor Syvertson had absolutely insisted I have it with me or I wouldn't get paid, but he didn't argue when I said I wouldn't wear it in sight.

I asked Gus if old Foote had ever stuck his nose in the beer parlor and he said never.

'How about Arhart, the jeweler?'

'Don't make me laugh. That stiff-necked son of a bitch wouldn't go into a soda parlor.'

I thought about that awhile and when I'd warmed up enough started up the west hill and after three blocks' hike was rapping on the jeweler's door. It took a while for him to answer and when he did he took his time getting the inner door and the storm open and he scowled at his watch and then at me and wanted to know what I was doing pounding doors at this time of night?

'I'm investigating a murder and as the town cop I'm here to ask you about the victim. You gonna let me in or do I get a court order?'

Having power and using it is almost as good as drinking booze. Arhart's mouth dropped open, he stepped back and I shoved past into the warmth of the dark hall, stamped my feet on his rag rug, gave them an extra swipe and moved into his parlor.

Mrs. Arhart looked up from a magazine and actually smiled. She was a plump, comfortable sort of woman with a firm chin, round cheeks, a nose the size of a cherry but not so red and dimples you could hide a blueberry in. Her hair was still mostly blonde with just flecks of gray.

Suddenly the smile faded and she took on a worried look.

'How's your father?' she asked.

'He's resting quiet,' I said. I didn't ask how she knew; in Corden, news travels faster than sound.

She invited me to take off my coat and sit down and asked would I like coffee? I turned that down to be polite and she ignored the refusal and got up to make some. Arhart took his corner chair and sat, looking sullen.

'Foote hasn't worked for me in over five years,' he said, 'I don't see what you expect from me.'

'Not much. Why'd you let him go?'

'I didn't have any choice. Times were

27

turning bad, I didn't have work for him. Besides, after the fire and all, he wasn't worth his hire. Just moped. I kept him on for six months or more and then had to stop it. There was no choice.'

'He was okay before the fire?'

'He was all right.'

'Was he a good watchmaker?'

'Yes, actually, he was. Slow but sure. Never missed a day.'

'You ever talk to each other about anything personal?'

He looked as if the notion gave him a bad taste in the mouth.

'No,' he said, shaking his head. 'We had no time for that.'

Mrs. Arhart came in with coffee and her husband settled back in his chair, holding his cup and withdrawing. He expected her to handle the social amenities and she did it naturally, asking about Ma and how things were at the hotel. She inquired about Joey and finally asked how I liked being a policeman.

I confessed it was an unnatural role.

'But you are rather enjoying it, aren't you?'

'It has its moments,' I confessed. 'You worked in the store now and then, didn't you. How'd you like Foote?'

'His name was Arthur,' she told me firmly, 'and I felt very sorry for him. He lived a tragic life.'

28

'He tell you about it?'

'A little. His wife died when their house burned, you know. She and the baby. The poor little thing didn't even have a name.'

'Where was her family—the rest of them?'

'Well, Kitty was at the dance at the Playhouse, and Buff was at a movie. Arthur was just, well, off somewhere. He took long walks, you know.'

'Did he talk about his family any before the fire?'

'No, I can't say he did. I'd ask him, you know, how the children were doing and how was his wife. I always felt he was terribly proud of them but too shy to say so.'

'Wasn't she a lot younger than him, the wife, I mean?'

'Yes,' she nodded. 'Over ten years, I'd judge. She was a pretty little thing, wonderful eyes, slim and quick. Lots of folks wondered how she happened to marry Arthur. I suspect a young man disappointed her and she wanted to marry someone safe and gentle.'

'Anyone ever have reason to think she got interested in a younger fella?'

Her answer came a little slow and I thought when she made it she was trying to come on strong so I wouldn't notice.

'No—not at all. She was a religious girl, you know. Sang in the choir. Had a voice like an angel. She just wasn't the sort of girl to be foolish.'

I knew from experience that a choir girl wasn't always a virgin, but it didn't seem appropriate to discuss that point with Mrs. Arhart.

'I didn't know she sang,' I admitted. 'Did she have friends in the choir?'

'I imagine so. Actually she dropped out quite a while back. I guess she was busy with the children and all and when she got pregnant the last time she just sort of withdrew.'

'Did you know about the check Arthur got every month?'

'Oh, yes, I heard about it, but he never said anything and I certainly didn't ask. I don't think it could've amounted to much, not the way he lived.'

'But he owned the house that burned?'

'Yes. That was completely lost, of course, in the fire. He told me it wasn't insured. He didn't believe in insurance. That was an awful shame. He just lost everything all at once. We took them in for a while, you know. Arthur and the two remaining children. Then Kitty went off to stay with her aunt in Aquatown and Buff joined the navy.'

I asked how they got along as a family while they were living in her house. She got defensive, said there was no way to judge that, the circumstances weren't normal and they were numb from the shock of losing Azalea and the baby and their home all at

30

once. I tried to press her a little on whether either of the kids had been a problem, but she brushed me off and tried to pump me about my romantic interests and general travels. I gave her some of the travels and none of the romance and finally thanked them both and went back out in the cold.

CHAPTER FOUR

Kitty showed up Wednesday afternoon. I'd spent most of the day messing with chores at the hotel since Elihu was still flat on his back and Ma, who's one of those people that never gets sick, was having trouble coping with the notion that he wouldn't be up any minute, bitching about when do we eat or demanding to know where was his screwdriver?

Even Bertha, our two-ton cook, was stunned and moved around her kitchen with a vague, preoccupied stare. She overcooked my breakfast eggs, underdid the toast and made coffee strong enough to use for varnish remover. When I tried to kid her, she just stared at me like a stunned ox.

I closed the dining room after a disastrous lunch hour and got her to nap until four. By four-thirty we were sitting beside the windows overlooking the snow-filled backyard and I was trying to get her thinking about making dinner when the lobby bell clanged.

When I entered the office alcove in the lobby, Kitty was bending over the register and all I could see was her small fur cap and black hair around it. She heard my step and glanced up. Her brown eyes had flecks of gold and stared at me from under black eyebrows. Her lashes seemed long enough to brush a man's cheek from a foot away.

'If you're a cop,' she said, 'where's your badge?'

'In my shirt pocket. I'm an undercover man.'

'Uh-huh. From what I've heard, undercover work is your speciality all right. Got a room for me?'

'If I didn't, I'd make one. You got over your cold?'

'Yeah.'

She looked down, added her address behind her signature with a small, firm hand and straightened up. She was wearing a fur-collared coat that matched the hat and looked like a Hollywood Gypsy.

'I thought you'd be getting gray,' she said.

'Haven't felt the obligation yet. What'd you do, marry money?'

'Not directly. It's usually on the far side of a man.'

'Except when the woman outlives him.'

'Well, I haven't yet, but all things come to

32

her who waits, right?'

I took her up to fourteen just at the top of the stairs and to the right, real handy to the shower on the left and the toilet down the hall.

'You keep it cold enough,' she said as she walked to the center of the room and wheeled slowly, taking in the spare furnishings and the vertical-striped wallpaper.

'No, the winter does that. We just fight it with fire and figure we're ahead if the water doesn't freeze in your pitcher.'

She removed her hat, tilted her head back and shook her hair. It was short and shiny with a fresh-washed look.

'Who's got Arthur?'

For a second I didn't realize she meant her father, then I remembered Mrs. Arhart calling him that.

'Scanlon's,' I said. 'He's the only undertaker we got, remember?'

'No. I never had any interest in things like that.'

She stood by the bed, peeling off her gloves, glanced at the single window and moved over to pull down the shade. Then she turned and fired her eyes at me.

'You want to talk or are you waiting for a tip?'

'Both.'

She grinned and I gave it back.

'You run the hotel now?'

33

'I'm just helping out while Elihu's down.'

'What do you mean, down? Sick?'

'Had a stroke last night.'

'How awful—is he in the hospital?'

'Nope. Downstairs in his room.'

She decided it was no big deal, lost interest, moved over to the bed, sat down and bounced once.

'Well, innerspring mattress, right?'

'Uh-huh. We've got five of them now.'

'My, my. Next you'll have wash basins with hot and cold running water in every room I suppose.'

'We already got it in number ten. I'd have given you that but Doc Obespi the foot man's got it through tomorrow.'

'He's still coming around? What, twice a year to take care of all the old ladies' bunions and corns? Now there's a job for you. Imagine spending all day bending over old ladies' gnarled feet.'

'I'd rather not, thanks. You know where your pa's monthly check came from?'

She tilted her dark head and lifted her chin.

'Yeah, Aberdeen. Why?'

'I know it was from a bank there, but who set it up, how come he got it?'

She shook her head slowly, leaned back against her propped arms and said, 'You got me. As long as I can remember it just came. I guess I used to think everybody got a check in the mail on the first of the month.'

'The aunt you went to stay with in Aquatown, was she your pa's sister, or your mother's?'

'Mom's. Arthur didn't have any family living that I know of.'

'You know what started the fire that burned your house?'

'Somebody said it was just a chimney fire. It happens all the time when people don't clean out the gunk that builds up.'

'I hear you were at the dance that night.'

'Yeah,' she leaned forward and rested her elbows on her silk-stockinged knees. 'I'll tell you, Carl, that's not my favorite night to remember. I don't want to talk about it and I can't think of any reason you'd be nosy about it, so the hell with it, okay?'

I said sure, sat down on the straight chair beside the marble-topped dresser and rolled a smoke. She watched, tilting her head so her cheek brushed the fur collar. The wind moaned, sharpened to a whistle and faded away.

'I can't really believe you're a cop,' she said.

'I can't either. You want a smoke?'

'Why not?'

I rolled another, gave us both a light and leaned back. She inhaled real easy and let it out in a smooth stream.

'How come you never call Foote your

father?'

She took a deeper drag on the cigarette and stared at me through the smoke she let out through her fine nostrils. After a moment she said, 'He wasn't my father.'

When I nodded, she frowned.

'He wasn't Buff's father either.'

'How about the baby?'

She looked down at her cigarette. 'I'm not so sure about that.'

'How come you're so sure about you and Buff?'

'All you've got to do is look at me for God's sake. Black hair, brown eyes. Ma was blonde and blue-eyed, Arthur, when he had hair, was sandy and his eyes were gray.'

'That's not absolute proof.'

'Maybe not. But it made me wonder early on and I finally asked Ma. She didn't admit it right away, but I kept at her and after a while she admitted he wasn't the one. She said my real pa was a very important man. She was proud of that.'

'She tell you anything about him?'

She examined her hands for a few seconds. I couldn't decide whether she thought she'd made a mistake in what she'd already said or was deciding just how far she could go in kidding me along. Finally she smiled, looked up and shrugged her shoulders.

'I'll tell you, Carl, we talked about that when I was awfully young and while I seem to

36

remember it like yesterday, I'm not real sure now if what she said is what I remember. She talked about him having a great mission and her being too young and he was married and would be ruined if he got a divorce to marry Ma. At the time it seemed awfully romantic and now it just sounds sad and stupid. She married Arthur because she was pregnant and he loved her and didn't care who'd had her first if he could have her last.'

'So your mother got together with this guy again and had Buff, after she married Arthur?'

'She never admitted that to me, but yes, I think that's what happened. It's pretty vague in my memory, but I seem to remember she went on sudden trips several times. It was supposed to be visits to relatives who needed her. I know Arthur always got horribly quiet when she was away like that and when I asked him why she left us alone he'd sit with me and tell me how wonderful she was and that lots of people needed her and I should understand and be unselfish.'

She looked at me with hard eyes that warned against my cracks about such foolishness. I met her stare and nodded.

'When she was home, how'd they get on?' I asked.

She fingered her fur collar and I saw the diamond glittering on her left hand.

'They got on okay. She mother-henned him

some and he fussed over her. They didn't talk a whole lot—I mean, no real conversation about anything. It was mostly, "Please pass the sugar," and "Do you want me to buy milk?" That kind of thing. They didn't either one of them read newspapers and gab about news. Hell, they didn't even gossip about the neighbors. I remember when she first got pregnant with the baby she quit singing in the choir and there was some talk about that. Arthur was upset. He loved her singing. So she told him, I'll sing at home, but she hardly ever did.'

'Did she go on a trip before getting pregnant the last time?'

'I don't really remember. That probably means she didn't because by then I should've been old enough to notice. Maybe not. I was already getting very interested in boys and stuff.'

I asked if she knew anything about her grandparents or other relatives and she said no, except for the aunt in Aquatown. Her mother had been orphaned in her teens and was raised by a family in town who had quite a bit of money and treated her like a servant. Foote's mother had died in childbirth trying to deliver a second son and his father had been killed during an attempted robbery in the jewelry store he owned.

'And Arthur had inherited the store?'

She said yes. It was just a little store. I

asked if it were possible the father had left a trust for Arthur.

'You mean, could the checks have come from that? I suppose it's possible, but it hardly seems likely. The store was never much and after Arthur took over it never made money. He had to give up after a few years and then moved to Corden.'

'Why here?'

'I don't really know.'

'Was it right after he married your mother?'

'I think so.'

I asked if the aunt she'd stayed with was an older sister to Azalea and she said no, she'd been about a year younger. She too had been passed on to a well-fixed family but had been formally adopted and wound up marrying fairly well.

We had a second cigarette before I got around to asking Kitty if she'd ever had reason to think her mother messed around with men besides the guy she thought had fathered her and Buff. She tried to act shocked at the notion at first, then admitted she found it hard to believe there hadn't been at least some flirtations. As she said, Azalea was a very attractive and romantic woman, and God knows Arthur had nothing to offer but big dog devotion.

'How come,' I said, 'you wear a thousand-dollar engagement ring and a dime store gold band?'

She looked at her left hand, spread the fingers, then made a fist and glanced up at me.

'Because I bought the band for this trip.'

'You're not married?'

'You got it.'

'I may have it, but I don't get it. Why?'

'I'm weird. Did you actually spend a year on the beach in the Philippines?'

'No, it was more like six months. Seemed less at first and more at last.'

'You got bored.'

'Yeah.'

She shook her head. 'And I thought *I* was weird. You got bored with the South Pacific and came back *here*?'

I allowed that was a little hard to figure.

She reached into her coat pocket, dug out a purse and found a quarter.

'Here's your tip. Good night.'

I scowled at the coin.

'What's the matter—isn't it enough?'

'I'm the town cop, I can't take dough from people I question. It wouldn't look good.'

'You're sore,' she said, looking pleased.

'Just wounded. Good night, Pussy Foote.'

She didn't throw anything or even growl; in fact, when I looked back before closing the door, I caught her grin.

CHAPTER FIVE

'Who was that?' Ma asked as I returned to the lobby.

'You know blamed well, she wrote her name on the register.'

She humphed and said I'd certainly spent long enough upstairs with her. I said that depended on what she meant "long enough" was for.

'You might ask about your father,' she said.

'I figure he's sleeping since you're out here.'

'He's sleeping comfortably, no thanks to you.'

I told her he'd be better off at the hospital, but what I meant was, she would be if he was. She ignored that and suggested I go tend the fires.

So I did. The hotel has two coal burners, the hot air job under the lobby and a boiler under the west wing. Elihu had installed the boiler about ten years after the first furnace and had to dig out a cellar to do it. To get to that one I had to hike across the back lot. The path was deep and packed hard as concrete. My boots slipped on its surface while the wind whipped around, smacking me in the face one minute and the butt the next. The sloping doors creaked as I lifted them up and I clattered down the steep steps, which creaked and popped under my weight. I snapped on the wall switch and fed the boiler chunks of lignite after shaking down the ashes and lifting out a big clinker with the iron tongs. It squatted in the iron tub beside the boiler and glowed fiercely.

I had hoped to see Kitty at supper but she didn't show up until well after we'd eaten. She stopped to tell me she'd gone over to Bond's Cafe just for old times' sake and hadn't seen anyone she knew well. Pretty soon she drifted up to her room.

After Ma went to bed a little past ten I turned out the lights except for the lamp on the registration counter and went to stand by the window beside the front door.

The city plow had raised snowbanks from two to three feet high along Main and the wind was hard at work flattening them out again. Blowing snow haloed our corner streetlight and turned those far away to a fuzzy glow.

I caught a flash of light off toward the east and watched it grow brighter, finally breaking into headlights that eased up the grade from the depot. They slowed to a crawl at our corner, passed on, made a wide, aborted U-turn and angle-parked facing the hotel. Before it turned I could see it was a black, four-door Packard. Its big tires laid deep, distinct tracks that quickly began filling.

The car lights glared through the north window, turning the lobby bright for several seconds, then abruptly shut off, leaving me blinking in the dark.

I walked over to the window and stared out. Nothing happened for several seconds. Then a match flared and I saw the driver twist around as a white face under a black hat came forward from the back seat. Slender hands cupped the light, which was suddenly gone and there was only the glow of a cigar end, which turned a deeper red as the smoker drew hard and leaned back.

The driver got out, stepped gingerly through the snow and opened the left rear door. The smoker emerged, wearing a black overcoat and overshoes. The driver stomped ahead to the corner, through the shoveled area and on up to the door with his boss close behind.

I rested my butt on the newspaper table under the wall clock and waited.

The smoker entered first followed by his driver, who pulled the storm door behind him and pushed the inner door shut firmly.

'Hi,' I said.

The driver started and whirled to face me. The smoker casually turned his head, taking aim with the cigar.

'We need two rooms,' he said.

I shoved off the table and went around

behind the registration counter. They approached me as I turned the register on its swivel. The smoker took off his wide-brimmed hat, handed it to his driver and moved into the light. His dark hair was flecked with gray and thinning at the crown. He placed the pen on the line under Kitty's name and paused for a second before writing John J. Johnstone in swooping loops. After entering a Minneapolis address he studied the register a moment, then handed the pen to his man and stepped aside.

'What's your name?' he asked me. The eyes peering out from under black, tufted brows were a hard blue.

I told him.

'You own this place?'

'It belongs to my old man.'

His man signed Jack O'Keefe in a crabbed hand and glanced at me with a measuring look. His eyes were cold, dark and mean. His nose was blunt as a hammerhead and he had high cheekbones and a clamped jaw. I returned his scowl and when it deepened, gave him my grin.

'If you don't have bags,' I said, 'you pay in advance.'

O'Keefe started to turn red but Johnstone nodded.

'We've got luggage. Go get it, Jack.'

Jack glared at me and went out. I told Johnstone he could hang his coat in the hall and he said no thanks, he'd keep it with him, so I led the way upstairs. He slowed a step as we passed room fourteen, where I'd put Kitty Foote, but said nothing and followed me down to seventeen. The door was open, as all doors are in the Wilcox Hotel until the rooms are occupied. I went in, snapped on the bed lamp and turned around. Johnstone looked at the brass bedstead, the marble-topped bureau with commode door and the big white pitcher in its matching white bowl reflected in the long bureau mirror.

'Where's the bath?'

'Back down the hall, turn right, first door on your left. The toilet's further down the hall, past the servants' stairs on the right.'

He didn't look overjoyed, so I didn't tell him he was in luck, during the winter the furnace heats our bathwater and he didn't have to pay a quarter extra for me to turn on the gas or wait half an hour for the water to warm up.

He tested the bedsprings, turned the covers back and said at least the place looked clean.

'You bet. We wash the linen every year. Never know when we might get royalty.'

He stared at me thoughtfully. Something about his big brow gave the impression he thought a lot. I didn't think it was much about philosophy or religion.

Then O'Keefe showed up carrying five bags with ease. He slipped through the door

45

like a wet snake and deposited his load on the floor. Johnstone took off his coat, handed it to O'Keefe, who looked around with elaborate care.

'You hang stuff on the wall pegs,' I said, pointing. 'Your room's across the hall.'

I wished them both good night and drifted toward the stairs. They both closed their doors. I moved in front of fourteen and tapped lightly.

After a second I heard her voice.

'Who?'

'Carl. Can I see you a sec?'

'What about?'

'A guy named Johnstone.'

She opened the door and stepped back. I walked past her, turned around and saw she was wearing a pink nightgown under a white robe.

She leaned against the closed door and said, 'What about a man named Johnstone?'

'I just put him in seventeen. He showed a lot of interest in your name on the register. Comes from Minneapolis. I thought maybe you knew him.'

She ambled over to the bed and sat down. 'Yeah. He's the guy I'm not married to.'

'Huh?'

'I've been living with him.'

'But you walked out?'

'That's about the size of it.'

'So what's he doing here?'

46

She glanced toward the door and shook her head. 'I don't know. He's too smart to think he can change my mind. On the other hand, he doesn't always act as smart as he is. Has he got Jack with him?'

I nodded and reached for my cigarette makings. She shook her head.

'Don't light up. I'm not going to let him in, but he might smell it from the hall.'

I put the fixings away and moved toward the door.

'Don't go yet,' she said. 'He always makes a last trip to the bathroom before bed. It wouldn't work out too great if he bumped into you coming out of my room.'

That made sense. It also made sense when she said she'd better turn off the light so when he went by he wouldn't get ideas. Of course I immediately started getting ideas. Especially when I heard the rustle of sheets as she slipped into bed.

I was still standing by the door when someone entered the hall from the west and walked our way. The steps halted outside fourteen.

I wished I'd asked Kitty if her man or his driver carried a gun.

There was a soft tap on the door.

Kitty ignored it.

The tap was repeated. Louder. I heard the covers rustle and the next moment Kitty was beside me at the door.

47

'Who is it?'

'Me. Open up.'

'Don't be silly. What do you want?'

'Are you alone?'

'No.'

That tears it, I thought.

After a couple of seconds' silence he asked who was with her.

'The Mormon Tabernacle Choir, you idiot—who'd you think?'

After another moment's silence he said, 'I want to talk with you. Let me in.'

'I know your kind of talk. You can see me in the morning if talk's what you're after. Now go to bed before you wake the whole damned place.'

'You've got no reason to be sore at me,' he said.

'I don't need a reason.'

He muttered something and a moment later went around the corner toward the bathroom.

Kitty expelled a deep breath, glided back to her bed and climbed in.

'Give you a scare?' she whispered.

'Yeah.'

She giggled.

'If I'd said yes, I'm alone, he'd have insisted I prove it. When I said I wasn't he was afraid to find out.'

'Has he caught you before?'

'Not a chance. I'm a good girl.'

I wondered what she was good at and

48

thought I could guess.

'What's Jack do besides drive his car and haul luggage?'

'Lots of things. He killed a man once.'

'For Johnstone?'

'Not the one I know about. But he'd do anything John asked. He was a union organizer once, then a cop. He was kicked off the police force in St. Paul because a prisoner he was supposed to be bringing in died from a beating during the arrest. Jack's very rough. I think he's a little crazy, but most of the time John can keep him under control.'

'What kind of business is Johnstone in?'

'Real estate and stuff.'

'It sounds more like stuff. Like bootlegging.'

'He was into that a while back. He still likes to think he's a racketeer but, really, he's mostly tame now. He was a marine too. A major. A very tough guy. That's what he likes to think.'

We heard him return from the bathroom and go by. He didn't even pause as he passed our door.

Jack made his trip and was much quicker than his boss.

Finally the hall was silent and I reached for the doorknob.

'What would you have done if he'd come in?' asked Kitty.

'We'll never know.'

'I guess you would've crawled under the bed, huh?'

'Not likely.'

She giggled again.

'You don't scare easy, do you? I've heard an awful lot about you, you know? You've got quite a reputation.'

'For what?'

'Lots of things. I heard you're good at about anything you try. Want to kiss me good night?'

I took a deep breath.

'What I'd really like to do is screw your brains out.'

'Well,' she said slowly, 'you could give it a try . . .'

So I did but as far as I could tell when I left her brains were still where they were when I started. It wasn't a failure that kept me awake.

CHAPTER SIX

I got up just after seven in a room as bright as noon because the sun reflecting on new snow sent its brightness through the window shade as if it weren't there.

It was nice to find the toilet water unfrozen when I hit the bathroom and from there I hiked, all booted, capped and jacketed, across the back lot to the west cellar, where I revived the banked fire till it was roaring, returned to the east furnace and did likewise.

Back in the kitchen Bertha was at work, red-faced and gimlet-eyed, so I knew the old man had survived the night. I didn't say anything because I'd learned long back I could tease her about anything but her love for that old bastard.

Daisy, the latest in our string of Norsky hired girls, was sitting at the kitchen table by the windows, sipping from a steamy cup when I came in. She gave me her blank, blue-eyed stare, then lowered her eyes quickly to the oilclothed tabletop.

'You know,' I said, 'now I'm the town cop you got to show respect and do as I say, don't you?'

She shook her yellow head.

'It's a fact,' I said.

'It's a goddamned joke,' said Bertha.

'You're not laughing.'

'It's not a funny joke. You, girl, when this one's around keep your legs crossed. He's quicker and slicker than a snake.'

I gave them up and went back to the lobby.

O'Keefe showed up and stood by the window just north of the front door, squinting out into the glare of sun and snow. His profile was all blunt lumps. Bulgy forehead, flat nose, jutting jaw. His high cheekbones looked like lumped muscle. He

51

wore a black suit, white shirt and blue tie with a big knot that was supposed to hide his unbuttoned collar. I guessed he had trouble finding shirts to fit around his thick neck.

He turned his narrow, cold eyes on me.

'They served breakfast?'

'Yup.'

He went back upstairs to fetch his master.

They were in a booth shoveling in eggs and bacon when Kitty came down and entered the lobby. She was in black but didn't look at all mournful.

She said good morning so casually nobody but me would've thought we hadn't shared anything cozier than a cup of coffee the night before. She asked me was it cold outside?

I said no, only about twenty below.

'Anybody else up?'

'If you mean Johnstone, yeah. So's his sidekick.'

She sighed, glanced out at the blinding glare of Main and blinked.

'Sleep okay?' I asked.

'I think I died for a while.' She gave me a sudden, coquettish grin and asked how about me?

'The same.'

'Well, we must chat again soon,' she said and floated into the dining room.

Before long I drifted back to the kitchen for a cup of coffee and saw her in a booth with Johnstone and O'Keefe. Johnstone

52

looked thoughtful, O'Keefe was watching Kitty and she was talking. She didn't glance my way as I passed.

Our last regular guest checked out a little after nine and after closing the door behind him I went into the hall and called Myrtle, our telephone operator, to ask if anything had happened during the night I should know about.

She said Carrie Jorgenson had died but she didn't think that was a police matter. I asked about Joey. She said that Ellie, his housekeeper, reported he'd had a bad night but had got to sleep finally and seemed to be resting okay.

'How's Elihu?' she asked.

'Spoiled rotten. Bertha brought him breakfast in bed.'

'You should talk more respectful, Carl. You've taken on responsibilities now, you can't just go on pretending to be a bum.'

Before I could begin a debate on that I had to break off because I heard the front door open and had to get back to the lobby.

I found a tall young man beside the door, pulling off gauntlet gloves and blinking. His eyes were watering.

He nodded to acknowledge my 'Hi' and concentrated on removing his overshoes, using the toe-to-heel technique. When that was accomplished, he ambled over to the registration desk and squinted at the names on the yellow sheet. After a moment he stepped back and stared down at the hot-air register under his feet.

'Now that's damn clever,' he said. 'You blow cold air through in the summer?'

'There's not enough summer to worry about. You here for the funeral?'

He raised his head carefully and took me in with his brown eyes.

'What funeral?'

'Fella named Arthur Foote.'

He glanced back at the names on the registration sheet.

'He somebody well known here?'

'Not very. Just an old fella that died. I thought you might be his son.'

'Really?' He stared at me. 'Do I look like him?'

'No. Not at all.'

'So why'd you ask was I going to his funeral?'

'That's the only action in town this weekend.'

He nodded as though that were quite logical, picked up the pen and slowly wrote Louis Link in the line under O'Keefe. He entered a St. Paul address and asked if the dining room was still open. I said he could probably at least get a cup of coffee.

After he'd hung his coat on a hall hook I walked him back to the dining room. Kitty and her friends were still in their booth and she was still doing the talking. O'Keefe turned and gave our new guest the cold eye. Unabashed, Link walked directly up to them.

'Good morning,' he said to Kitty. 'My name's Link. Louis Link. Haven't we met?'

Kitty's eyes opened wide, then quickly narrowed as she frowned thoughtfully.

'Could be—you from Minneapolis?'

'Close—St. Paul.'

She agreed that was close all right and asked if he'd care to join them. He said he'd be delighted and slid in beside her.

Johnstone was quite a study. He looked stunned at first, then turned red and finally became thoughtful. O'Keefe's eyes kept swinging from his boss to the intruder, looking for a signal.

Kitty asked Link if he'd been in town long and they began chatting as if they were alone at the table. I drifted back to the kitchen and sent Daisy to take the new guy's order. Then I went back to the lobby.

After a while the quartet straggled back through; first Kitty, with Link just behind, then Johnstone followed by O'Keefe. By this time Johnstone was looking casual as he puffed on a long cigar, but O'Keefe hadn't decided what he should do and it made him mad.

When Kitty went up to her room, Link said he was going up to his.

I watched Johnstone as they went. He sat

55

down in one of the rockers, leaned back and puffed calmly on his cigar. O'Keefe, looking bewildered, went over to the newspaper table and began shuffling through the ancient history.

'You notice anything special about that young fellow?' asked Johnstone, looking at me.

'Yeah. He seems to move faster than most.'

'Uh-huh. He also looks like Kitty. You notice that?'

I nodded.

'Like they were twins.'

'Not quite identical,' I said.

He gave me a smile that could sell skunk spray.

'She's got a brother, you know.'

'I know.'

'He says he's just got to town. You believe that?'

'Shouldn't I?'

'Her brother's supposed to be in the navy. But the last I heard, he's gone AWOL. You may be harboring a fugitive.'

'Not knowingly.'

'Wrong. I just told you.'

'Is that why you came to Corden? To fink on Kitty's brother?'

He blew out a cloud and watched it drift slowly north. Then he smiled at me again.

'I came to look after Kitty. She's mine, you know.'

'I didn't notice the collar.'

'You don't collar cats.'

'You don't own them either.'

He chuckled easily. 'You're right. I keep forgetting that.'

I asked if he'd known Kitty's pa and he said no, never met the man. No, she'd never talked about him until she said she was coming to his funeral.

'You know he was murdered?'

His sales grin disappeared and the broad face became blank. He shook his head slowly.

'He was beaten all to hell and hung with a barbed wire noose.'

Johnstone took the cigar from his mouth and studied me from under his dark eyebrows. 'No wonder she acted funny. You seem to be pretty much into all this—'

'I'm the temporary town cop.'

'You've got to be kidding.'

'Nope. Got the badge right here in my shirt pocket.'

'He's carrying a concealed weapon,' said O'Keefe.

Johnstone wiped out his grin with a glance and looked back at me.

'You're going to need help,' he said.

'Yeah. How long've you known Kitty?'

He pulled back a little, then said about four years.

'You're in real estate, huh?'

'I'm in a lot of things.'

'Which one of them makes you need a bodyguard?'

'None of them. And I can take care of myself. Jack drives my car and handles things for me. He's very handy. He used to be a cop. Was a marine before that.'

'In your outfit?'

He took a drag on the cigar and scowled at me.

'I guess you've been talking to Kitty.'

'Some.'

I was sure he wanted to ask if that'd been before or after he'd shown up, but he couldn't quite bring himself to know and slowly he leaned back in the rocker and smiled.

'I think,' he said, 'you could be an easy guy to underestimate.'

I smiled back.

'How'd you and Kitty happen to get together?' I asked.

'Isn't it obvious? She's rich and I'm beautiful.'

CHAPTER SEVEN

It had warmed to ten below by funeral time and thanks to an ambitious janitor's coal-shoveling the church was hot enough to hint what was in store for sinners in the next world.

Foote drew a sparse crowd, maybe a dozen old ladies, half as many old men and our gang from the hotel: Ma, Kitty, Link, Johnstone, O'Keefe and me.

It was my first trip to the Catholic church and Ma warned me to watch Kitty so I'd know the ups and downs and woudn't disgrace the family. Except for all the gewgaws and candles it wasn't much different from the Congregational church. The organ was just as bad. The priest's line was easier to take; he stuck to the subject and left out the hell and brimstone Clausen always throws in whenever he's got a captive audience.

Father Patterson tried to make something of Foote, but about all he could say was the man had meant well, died hard and God would have mercy. I agreed with the first two but had reservations about the mercy bit. When there's so little in life, it doesn't seem too likely there'll be much in the hereafter.

It felt good getting back out in the cold, clear air. There was no graveside ceremony, they had to wait for spring to dig the hole, so we all headed back to the hotel throwing eighteen-foot shadows made by the distant sun and felt the cut of the prairie winds swinging in sharp from the north. Snow squeaked under our feet and we squinted against the glare of sun and snow.

Back in the warm lobby Johnstone was

elaborately respectful toward Ma. They agreed the elegy had been tasteful and that Catholics certainly knew how to deal with occasions. Ma got so carried away she even admitted knowing a couple Catholics who were pretty decent people but confessed she'd never understood why they thought they had to go to mass at 6:00 A.M.

'They got a wild religion,' I said, 'they got to sneak up on it early.'

She gave me a dirty look, turned back to Johnstone and asked what church he went to. He warmed her with his smile and said he'd grown up a Methodist.

'You're saying you don't belong now, aren't you?'

She said it in a tone that suggested he was naughty and I realized she was flirting with him.

His smile broke into a chuckle. 'I don't think I said that at all—but you're right. I'll bet you don't miss a thing.'

Ma led us into the parlor and Daisy delivered coffee, sugar and cream on a tray and we helped ourselves to cups she'd set on the low bookshelf against the east wall. There was a lull while everybody sugared and creamed, stirred and sipped.

Kitty sat on the couch with Link on her left and looked thoughtful, maybe even melancholic. Link was broody and avoided looking at Johnstone or O'Keefe. Mostly he

60

eyed Ma and now and then he glanced my way. As general chatter got started his eyes turned mean and his wiry body twitched with impatience. Suddenly he broke through one of Ma's monologues.

'You think the old man was murdered?' he asked me.

'Where'd you get that notion?'

He slid back on the couch and looked into his cup.

'I heard something—'

'Where?'

'At the funeral. Or right after, when people were coming out.'

'Ah. How come you went to the funeral?'

He straightened, tried to smile and managed a smirk.

'You told me it was the only action in town.'

That didn't go over too big with the gathering and everybody looked my way with disapproval.

'You that hard up for entertainment?'

He glanced at Johnstone, then turned toward Kitty.

'I went because of her.'

'So you didn't have any personal interest, huh?'

He met my eyes straight on and said no.

I looked around. Everyone was watching him again. Johnstone frowned, O'Keefe was strictly deadpan, Kitty's mouth was open just

61

enough to show a glint of white teeth. Ma was tight-lipped with Puritan disapproval.

As I glanced back at Link the lobby door opened and closed. Ma glanced my way. I got up and went out to check.

A tall man stood by the front door, slowly unbuttoning a black overcoat. He nodded as I walked behind the registration counter and greeted him, stamped his feet, began unwinding his scarf and approached me.

'Cold out,' he said, pulling off his gloves.

His nose was wide and straight between tomato-red cheeks and his mouth looked like it'd been chopped out of marble. I told him where he could hang his coat and park his overshoes and once they were disposed of he came back and stood over the heat register, which stirred his blond hair. He rubbed his hands briskly, picked up the pen and signed Gregory Plant with a very elaborate hand, right under Link's signature.

I asked how long he planned to stay. He wasn't sure. He put down the pen and glanced at me. I got the feeling he wanted me to know he was amused and expected me to be offended by that.

I led him upstairs to six, which is straight back and just off an open square where the servants' stair comes up beside the toilet room right next to the linen closet.

He looked around his room with a superior expression, walked over to the window and bent down to peer out under the half-lowered shade.

'I don't suppose it looks any better in the summer,' he said.

'It usually looks warmer then. At least in July.'

'Yeah.' He straightened up and grinned at me. 'Where's Kitty Foote's room?'

'At the head of the stairs. You know her?'

'Yeah.' He didn't quite leer.

I told him where the toilet and shower were, went downstairs and was putting on my coat when the parlor party began breaking up. Link saw me and asked where I was going. I said to the post office.

He said he'd join me and a moment later we were bundled up and hiking along the white street. He edged close.

'You really the town cop now?'

'Temporary.'

'Boy, I can hardly swallow that.'

'I'll bet you can't. You remember when I was on the other side.'

He shot a glance at me over his collar and grinned.

'I never fooled you, did I?'

I shook my head.

'You going to turn me in?'

I shook my head again.

'I didn't think you would. Actually, that act back there was for the others. I didn't want old J.J.J. to know who I was.'

'What's the difference?'

'I don't know—I just wanted to make him look foolish. I did, too. You see how rattled he got when he thought I was moving in on Kitty?'

'You rattled him good,' I said.

'Damn right. Shit, he's old enough to be her father. And going around with that hood at his heels, like some cheap racketeer. Who the hell's he think he's fooling?'

'You think he's a crook?'

'Nah. He just wants people to think he's dangerous. All that marine shit, you know? What gripes me is, Kitty goes for that. She couldn't stand it that old Arthur was nothing. She always wanted somebody people looked up to ... hell ... that's not it either. I don't know ...'

'She wanted power, maybe?'

'Yeah, I guess that's more like it. She doesn't really give a damn about J.J.J., but that big act he puts on makes people sit up and take notice. I mean, people honest to God respect this dumb son of a bitch because they're scared of him and his goon. It's pitiful when you think about it. I'd rather see Kitty with a guy like you—'

'You're not too great on flattery,' I told him.

'Oh,' he brushed that off as I opened the post office door, 'I didn't mean it *that* way, but Christ!'

64

It wasn't as windy inside as out but didn't seem much warmer. I glanced through the cage bars at the counter window and saw Luke, the postmaster, wearing a heavy sweater and writing in a ledger. He glanced up, waved, did a double take when he saw my companion and got up to come over.

'Buff Foote,' he said. 'How's the sailor?'

'Pretend you don't know me,' said Buff, 'I'm AWOL.'

'No kidding? That why you're with the town cop?'

'He doesn't know who I am.'

'Oh, good. I suppose you came for the funeral, huh? Terrible thing...'

They talked some while I took a single letter from our box and stuck it in my pocket. A minute later we were back on the windy street.

'You didn't really come for the funeral,' I said. 'You were AWOL before he was killed. Or found.'

'That's right.' He ducked his head against the cutting wind.

'And you've got to know the MPs will be coming after you.'

'In the navy it's the SPs. And they don't come hunting, they just send a wire to the local law, which is you, and you'll tell 'em there's nobody here but us chickens.'

'You didn't know I was going to be the town cop.'

65

'Joey wouldn't have turned me in either.'

'Why'd you go AWOL?'

'Got into trouble.'

'Like what?'

He peeked over his collar at me and ducked low again.

'Slugged an ensign.'

'Why?'

'He tried to move in on my girl.'

'In a bar?'

'Uh-huh.'

'Since when do officers and enlisted men hang out in the same bars?'

'This one was off-limits to both of us.'

He kept not looking at me except for sneaky glances.

I stopped on the corner across from the hotel and faced him.

'You're handing me a line of crap. You knew the old man was dead, you knew Kitty was coming here for the funeral. How long you been in Corden?'

He took a deep breath and met my stare directly. 'I didn't kill him.'

'Did you want to?'

His eyes slid away.

'Why'd I want to do that?'

'I don't know, but you sure as hell weren't all busted up over his murder. You don't give a damn who did it, do you?'

'No, not really. He wasn't my father, or Kitty's either. He wasn't anything to me, one

66

way or another.'

'You grew up with him. He supported you and your mother. What's the matter, did he whale you, offer short rations, try to make your sister?'

He got the expression of a man with a gut ache and wouldn't look at me. 'Let's go inside, for Christ's sake. I'm freezing out here.'

I took his arm, turned him around and led him back to Bond's Cafe. A moment later we were hunched over the back booth table, drinking coffee from thick, white mugs.

I told him what Kitty had already told me and asked if his mother had ever told him who their father was. He shook his head and said she hadn't even admitted to him that Arthur wasn't his father. She never confided in him the way she did with Kitty.

'So what makes you so sure Kitty wasn't just making things up because she was ashamed of Arthur?'

'I felt it, long before she ever told me. He never liked me—'

'How many kids you ever know were pals with their old men?'

He said lots but couldn't name any.

'Most kids,' I told him, 'figure at some time their real parents were royalty or something. Hell, I always wanted to believe my real pa was Hoot Gibson or Tom Mix. Better yet, Will Rogers. The only trouble was, Ma never met any of them. You got a prospect for your real pa?'

He shook his head and drank coffee and looked like he wished it was hemlock.

'Tell me about Arthur. What do you remember him doing?'

'He sat around and smoked a corncob, ate oatmeal and soup. He slurped. When Ma got mad, he'd sneak out.'

'What made her mad?'

'She never said. She'd just get quiet. When she didn't talk, there wasn't any talk in our house except when Kitty was around.'

'If she just got quiet, what made you think she was mad?'

'Oh, I could tell. She'd never let him touch her. He didn't try many times, but when he did, she'd pull away.'

'She ever touch him?'

'I guess so, yeah? When he was at the table she'd put her hands on his shoulders. Sometimes she'd shove his hair back when it flopped on his forehead.'

He was silent for a moment.

'The way it was,' he said thoughtfully, 'was like old Arthur was an old smelly dog that was yours and you felt sorry for him but kind of wished he'd die so you'd be shut of him.'

'You think Kitty hated him?'

'Kitty? Hell, no, she never hated anybody. She could see a warthog wallowing in shit and she'd say it was okay. She wouldn't admit he

68

stank.'

'You ever figure out how come your ma and this guy got married to each other?'

'Sure. She got pregnant by a married guy or something and had to marry somebody and Arthur was the only creep who'd take a pregnant woman.'

'You ever think he was maybe hired to marry her?'

'That's the silliest goddamned thing I ever heard. He was tickled to death to marry her—she was beautiful—'

'You said only a creep'd marry a pregnant woman.'

'Well, I said that because he was the way he was. Anybody would've been glad to marry her.'

'Except the guy that got her pregnant.'

'Well, there was a good reason, you can bet on that.'

'It'd sure help if I could find out who it was.'

'I don't see how that'd help.'

I wasn't sure how either, except that I needed just about any kind of information about the family to dope out why Foote had been killed in that especially mean way. I couldn't get away from the notion that whoever killed him had been after information. That the beating was to extort something the killer thought he had to know. Except what in hell could a nobody like Foote know that would be any earthly use to anybody? I told myself to quit trying to fancy things up, the killing was more likely a sadist's revenge.

I was still mulling that over while Buff sat gloomily staring into his coffee when the front door opened and Mayor Syvertson came charging in. He spotted me and hurried to sit down beside Buff without even glancing at him.

'I called Aberdeen,' he told me. 'Couldn't get the bank president, he's off to Minneapolis or someplace. The person I talked to wasn't the least bit respectful—'

'Probably figured you were only the town cop.'

'No,' he shook his head. 'I identified myself unmistakably and stated my reasons for calling in specific detail. There was absolutely no excuse...'

He went on quite awhile before noticing Buff for the first time and suddenly ran down and squinted at him.

'Who're you?' he demanded, then, realizing he sounded rude, managed a smile. 'I'm Mayor Syvertson.'

'Hi, Mayor,' said Buff soberly. 'My name's Link. M. Link. Everybody calls me M.'

The mayor looked doubtful. 'You don't live in Corden, do you?'

'Just passing through. Fine town. Garden spot.'

Syvertson forgot the slights he'd suffered from the Aberdeen bank employee and began to beam.

'You should see the town in summer. We've got more trees than any other place in South Dakota that doesn't have a river and the dandiest Fourth of July celebration too . . .'

He went on to explain we had the county seat and the newest theater and our football team had been undefeated through its last season. But pretty soon he ran out of gas and started remembering his snub and decided he had to go home and tell his wife about it.

When he was gone Buff shook his head and asked how that dumb turd got to be mayor. I said because nobody else wanted the job.

As we got up and started back toward the hotel he thanked me for not tipping off Syvertson. 'That son of a bitch wouldn't've waited a second to turn me in, even if he had to pay for the telephone call.'

'You remember him, huh?'

'Hell, yes, the stuffed shirt. He was bad before, but being mayor's made him worse.'

'I don't suppose being mayor has ever improved anyone a whole lot.'

We moved out on the walk and got belted by the wind as we turned west for the hotel.

'I got to ask,' I said. 'The M you said was your name, I suppose that's for Missing?'

'You got it,' he said and giggled.

71

I said I was afraid so and only hoped it wouldn't be fatal. We walked the rest of the way in silence.

CHAPTER EIGHT

Boswell was parked in the rocker next to the register cove when we came in; he smiled benevolently and greeted us both by name. I could see that shook Buff a little and when we were back hanging up our coats in the hall I told him the old man was probably the only party in town who'd ever talked much with Arthur Foote. He gave me a so what? look, but as soon as we moved into the lobby he took the rocker beside Boswell and turned sociable. After a little weather talk he asked what he and Arthur Foote had talked about when they got together.

'He talked about you and Kitty. Sometimes your ma.'

'Really?' Buff twisted around. 'You're not just saying that?'

'He talked about the weather some,' Boswell confessed.

Buff waved impatiently. 'What'd he say about us?'

'When you was a baby, he could flip the nipple out of your mouth and you'd just grin and grab it back.'

Buff flushed and turned away. I looked out the front window.

'What else?'

'He said the first time you stood by yourself you was so excited you crowed like a rooster.'

'Did he say anything about when I was older?'

Boswell thought about that and finally admitted no. Mostly Arthur seemed to think of the kids when they were little.

Buff squirmed and asked what he'd said of their mother.

'He said she was awful pretty, a grand cook and a fine mother.'

'She *was* a good cook, when she wanted. And she never whaled us.'

'Did *he*?' I asked.

Buff frowned, annoyed by the intrusion, and shook his head.

'He never paid me that much attention.'

That was said with such bitterness it worried Boswell.

'What'd Arthur say about Kitty?' I asked and got a scowl from Buff.

Boswell smiled and tilted the rocker back. 'He said she was just about the cutest little gal ever. Feisty as a wildcat, but a cuddler too. Used to sit in his lap and pull his tie.'

'I don't remember her ever doing that,' said Buff.

'Well, that was probably before you was old enough to notice.'

73

'I never saw her act like she wanted him to touch her. Not ever.'

'Well,' said Boswell, 'that's how little girls go when they get big.'

'No,' said Buff, shaking his head violently. 'He lied. She never sat on his lap—that's a goddamned lie.'

Boswell shrugged sadly.

'He lied,' insisted Buff, getting up so fast the rocker banged back. 'He lied about Ma too. He said she was bad—'

He saw me staring at him and got more excited than ever.

'He never respected Ma or gave a damn about us—it's all a lot of bullshit!'

Boswell looked at me as the young man stomped out and ran up the stairs.

'He asked,' said Boswell.

'He did. Don't worry about it. He's worked up his own notions about Foote and he can't handle any confusion about it right now.'

Boswell stared down at the pipe cradled in his thick hands.

'I didn't tell him how his pa said he sucked his thumb or that Kitty wet the bed.'

'I'm glad. That really would've made him go nuts. How'd you ever happen to get gassing with Foote?'

'It just happened,' he said, getting out his tobacco. 'He used to walk the railroad tracks and so did I. We passed each other a coupla times and this one day a freight came by just about when we met and we both stopped off to the side like and watched her go by and I asked about the kids and we got talking. He wasn't a fella to go on much.'

It was easy to picture. Boswell, once he made contact, was the kind who talks only enough to draw poeple out. His account of the meeting with Foote was the longest speech I'd ever heard from him.

'What'd you think about Foote?' I asked.

'Nice fella.'

'Ever meet anybody who wasn't?'

He nodded, tamped down the tobacco in his pipe and hauled out a match. 'That Murdock fella.'

'You still hold it against him just because he killed a few folks and tied you up?'

'He was bad.'

'Name another.'

He thought for a while before I told him to forget it, the strain was too much.

'When you talked with Foote, did he ever ask you any questions?'

He shook his head.

'You think he might not have been the pa of those two kids?'

'He *said* he was.'

I stared at him. With Boswell you can't ever be really sure there's all that innocence that seems to spread all over his wrinkled face.

'He said, "my Buff" and "my Kitty," so they were his as far as you're concerned?'

He nodded. All the thinking had distracted him, so the pipe died and he spent a few seconds getting it fired up again. Then he asked how Elihu was doing.

'Bitching about his feed, so I guess he's coming around. Did Foote ever say anything about the death of his wife and baby?'

He shook his head. 'He never talked about nothing I didn't ask and I left that alone.'

'You ever hear anybody else talk about the fire and all?'

'Sure. Folks didn't talk about much else for a month.'

'How'd they say it started?'

'Chimney. Folks said Arthur'd mentioned once the chimney'd oughta be cleaned.'

'Who said that? From all I've heard it seems blamed unlikely Foote'd be talking about a thing like that to anybody.'

He thought that over and slowly nodded his head.

'That's right. Never thought about it before. Don't remember where I heard the story—it just went around, you know?'

'Ever hear about fights between Foote and his wife?'

He hadn't. I asked what she looked like. He said she was small, slim and twitchy as a red squirrel. Bright black eyes, lots of dark hair. He'd never spoken to her and didn't

76

know if she'd had any close friends. Went to church and sang in the choir awhile but quit when she got pregnant the last time.

I asked if Father Patterson had been her priest. He said yes.

It was late afternoon when I climbed the northeast hill to the priest's house. The sun had just dropped under the horizon and dark was moving in from the east, cold as Eskimo death.

Old Sadie Grant answered my knock and fussed over me being out in such cold weather. I asked why wasn't she home and snug.

She laughed. 'The father'd starve if I didn't fix his dinner, and who'd I confess my neglect to if he was gone?'

'You could skip the middleman and go straight to the top.'

'You! You're just awful, Carl Wilcox. What're you here for? Planning to convert?'

I said I wanted to talk with him about a former member of his church.

'He won't tell you a thing,' she said with great satisfaction. 'Father Patterson never speaks of his people once they're gone.'

She took my coat, gave me a broom to brush off my boots and led me into the living room, where I found the father parked in an easy chair in his shirtsleeves and without a collar. He looked so human I felt like I had the wrong fellow for a moment, but he smiled

77

and invited me to sit down in his best fatherly manner.

'I understand you're the law in Corden now,' he said, as if the notion wasn't the least bit ridiculous.

'Not all of it. Joey's still alive, just a little inactive.'

'Well, I hope you appreciate the responsibility. I'd like you to know I fully endorse the mayor's choice under the circumstances. What do you want from me?'

He looked so fatherly and sounded so patronizing I was tempted to ask if he'd take my confession, but something in his clear blue eyes made me feel he didn't have the constitution for my load of sins, so I explained I was trying to get some notion about what the Foote family had been like.

'I didn't know Arthur well,' he said, sitting back and folding his hands. 'Azalea was a regular at mass and choir for a time. Had a voice like an angel. Never missed confession.'

'She have that much to confess?'

He gave me a stern frown.

'I'm afraid we won't be able to discuss that.'

'I didn't figure we would. But I need to find out what went on. She was young and pretty, he was old and ugly. How'd it work out?'

'Quite well.'

I stared at him awhile and he tried to smile

but after a bit stirred uncomfortably and sobered.

'She was a good woman,' he said irritably. 'She cared about her children and she sang in the choir, took care of her home and her husband—'

'And made trips out of town every now and then, right?'

He hunched forward, stared down at his hands a moment, looked up and sighed.

'Yes, she did.'

'Where?'

He settled back once more and rested his hands on the chair arms.

'I believe she said there was a cousin somewhere in the east.'

'You're saying that's where she went?'

He met my gaze directly.

'That's what she told everyone.'

'Except you.'

'She didn't go often. Not more than three or four times all told. She needed to get away. It was good for her.'

'But on the last trip she got pregnant, right?'

'We'll never know. The two people who could tell you are both gone.'

'There's a third party who isn't. That's the one I'm after.'

'I'm sorry, I can't help you there.'

'Okay,' I said and settled back in my chair. 'How about the kids, were they good

Catholics?'

He smiled sweetly. 'I like to think all Catholics are good ones but have to confess they didn't attend mass regularly, or confession either. Buff came a few times before he joined the navy.'

'You think he had problems?'

'He was an extremely sensitive, moody young man. Rebellious, often sullen. But somehow, I believe in my heart, he'll eventually return to the church.'

'How about Kitty?'

He shook his head. 'I'm afraid she's not a spiritual child.'

'She's not a child at all anymore.'

'That's true. Perhaps she never was.'

He liked that line and watched to see if I was savoring it.

'Kitty says Arthur wasn't her pa—or Buff's either.'

He lifted his eyebrows. 'Really? She told you that?'

He was trying to look skeptical, but I was sure he'd learned it all in the confessional with Azalea.

'Buff says Kitty told him Azalea was pregnant with her when she married Arthur—that the real father paid Arthur to marry her and take her away.'

'That sounds a bit fanciful.'

'Yeah. But Arthur got a monthly check from the time they moved here till the day he died.'

'Yes, I heard about that. Corden has few kept secrets.'

'Especially from priests, huh?'

'I don't know everything,' he said and I could tell he resented that.

'You know more than you're telling me. The fact is, I need help. I've got to know what's under the rocks and behind the walls—everything possible about that family.'

He gave me his fatherly smile.

'Ah, you need help. That's a new role for you, isn't it? From all I've ever heard, you never felt the need for succor, let alone asked for it.'

'This isn't personal.'

'A fine point. Very good.' He nodded, formed a steeple with his fingers and closed his eyes for a second.

'All right. I'll make just a little confession and hope you'll appreciate the uniqueness of our circumstances; I never really learned much about the Foote family. They were, and remain, one of my failures. I have more than I normally admit, but this was more poignant than most because I felt, many times, that I might reach Azalea. She was a very sensitive, spiritual woman. Several times, at confession, I felt she was on the verge of truly confiding in me, but she never managed, she always held back something—'

'Was she a born Catholic or a convert?'

81

He gazed at me thoughtfully.

'What makes you ask that?'

'I figure a born Catholic'd be used to unloading everything, while a convert might still hold out now and again.'

'That's not necessarily true. Converts are often much more totally Catholic than those born to it.'

'Okay, you think she wanted to confess to adultery?'

'Really, Carl, you know I'm not going to tell you anything like that. She was deeply disturbed and that's all I can say.'

'You think she could've set her own house on fire to commit suicide?'

He shuddered and shook his head. 'I can't believe that.'

He didn't want to believe it, but I was convinced the notion had crossed his mind and haunted him.

'How about Arthur? He ever come to confession?'

'Never.'

'To mass?'

'No.'

'Maybe he wasn't a Catholic at all.'

'Oh, yes. He wore the cross and, besides, Azalea told me he was born Catholic. He simply lost the light. I went around to visit their home once, hoping to get acquainted with him, but as soon as I entered, he excused himself and left. I told him that he was the one I wanted to talk with and he said, with an apologetic smile, that he didn't doubt it but when he wanted to see me he knew where I lived and until then we had nothing to talk about. I was shocked. I'm not used to such treatment, as you might guess. I told him I'd forgive him and hoped God would too and he simply nodded and went out the door.'

'How'd Azalea react to that?'

'She was very put out.' He laughed sheepishly. 'At the time I assumed she shared my anger with her husband. Later I realised her anger wasn't with him. I shouldn't, of course, have implied that I could be more patient and forgiving than God.'

'I never got the notion from my Bible reading that God was patient *or* forgiving. I figured that was Jesus's department.'

For a few seconds he considered whether it'd be fruitful to debate theology with an agnostic, then his expression became amused and he shook his head.

'Let's confine our discussion to the Foote family. If we enter into religious questions you'll be here all night.'

But our discussion of the Foote family made no more progress, so I thanked him after a while and left.

Outdoors was ghostly white under a bright, full moon and I figured South Dakota must be ungodly blinding if you looked down at it from up there. My creaking steps echoed over the white silence and I could see into houses along the way where people were moving toward their dining tables or sitting in living rooms waiting for the call. Somewhere, far off, I heard the grinding of a starter, over and over, more and more faint and halting. It had died by the time I crossed the street to the hotel.

I opened the storm door against the north wind and leaned into it as I unlatched the inner door, stepped inside and let it slam behind me. Johnstone, O'Keefe and Old Boswell were parked in rockers and all stared at me. The room was filled with the smells of roast beef, fried onions and Boswell's pipe.

'Mayor Syvertson called,' said Boswell. 'Wants you should ring him back.'

I went around to the hall behind the lobby, hung up my coat and rang the operator over the wall phone beside the safe.

Syvertson asked in his fussy voice where in the world I'd been, then didn't listen for an answer.

'I got through to the bank president in Aberdeen,' he told me. 'That trust was set up by a lawyer named Grover Plant. I called him and he admits he did it for a client but won't say who. Says that's confidential and privileged.'

'You threaten him with a court order?'

'I was going to, but he told me not to even try, I'd never get it. I've talked with our city

84

attorney, Al Jones, and he's not sure. Says he'll do some reading, but he thinks this Plant fellow's probably right.'

'Plant's first name was what?'

'Grover. Like in Cleveland, the president.'

'How old you figure he is?'

'I've no idea. Where'd you say you were when I called before?'

'Father Patterson's place.'

'Why the devil—excuse me—would you be talking to him?'

'I figured I was overdue for confession.'

'You're not Catholic.'

'That's what made me so overdue.'

He enjoyed that in injured silence. Then he said, 'You weren't fool enough to think he'd tell you anything Azalea said in confession, were you?'

'It seemed worth a shot. Actually I just figured he might know something about the family. It turns out he either doesn't or isn't saying.'

'It might have been quite a shock for him to find you at his door.'

'Not at all. He even claims he approves of your appointing me temporary chief.'

He never questioned the idea and was so tickled pink I knew he'd be calling Father Patterson to discuss it at tiresome length. It took me a while to get him back to the trust. I said there was something blamed fishy about it because sure as hell if it came from Arthur's old man there'd be no reason for his lawyer to get cagey about it.

That made Syvertson unhappy again. He didn't want to think about complications. Finally he said he guessed it was such a cold night there'd be no point in me making my rounds because nobody would start any trouble. I agreed.

And, of course, we were both wrong.

CHAPTER NINE

I asked Bertha if it was okay for Boswell to stay for dinner. She told me one more bum wouldn't make any difference, so I let him know and at six sharp we all trooped into the dining room and sat down around the big table like a boardinghouse gang.

Ma was eating in Elihu's room, which put me in the old man's chair. I felt like an imposter and forgot to introduce everybody. Kitty came in a couple minutes late and sat on my right. Buff was on her right and next to him was Gregory Plant.

When I'd downed enough of Bertha's pork roast and gravy I began to feel civil and looked over at Plant.

'Your name's familiar—you in the law business?'

He gave me a sly grin and shook his head.

'Where you from?'

'I wrote that down on the register.'

'Yeah. Minneapolis. But were you born there?'

'Is that what you're supposed to write on the register? Where you were born?'

By this time everybody was staring at him and he was enjoying it. I saw Kitty lean forward to look past her brother at him. She abruptly stopped chewing and stared hard.

'I wondered,' I said, 'if you might be related to a lawyer named Grover Plant.'

'He's my uncle,' he said and tipped his head forward to grin at Kitty.

Johnstone, who was sitting across from Plant, saw her expression and suddenly became very thoughtful.

'You're Gregory,' said Kitty accusingly.

Plant's grin broadened. He was so tickled I thought he was going to giggle, but he recovered, nodded and said, 'That's right, I saw a notice in the paper about your dad's death. Thought I'd come for the funeral but didn't quite make it on time.'

'Your uncle,' I said, 'was the guy who set up a trust for Kitty's pa some years back, when he was living in Aberdeen.'

'Right. And later on, Kitty came and boarded at our house when she started going to teacher's collage.'

'And you got to know each other?'

'Not much. I was going to the U at

Minnesota.'

'But you came home for vacations?'

Plant grinned at Kitty again and nodded. She gave him a long, hard stare, then deliberately picked up her knife and fork and resumed eating. At the same time Johnstone's appetite deserted him. Without looking her way he said, 'I don't remember your ever mentioning this fellow.'

'He was never anything to talk about.'

Johnstone glanced at her, looked back at Plant and rested his forearms on the table edge.

'At that time, what were you in college?'

Plant grinned at him. 'Senior. I was four years older than her. How much older are you?'

Johnstone's responding smile wasn't happy or friendly.

'This fellow's quite the gentleman,' he said to Kitty.

'He wears shoes,' she said.

After taking a drink of coffee she crossed her knife and fork on her plate, pushed her chair back, smiled at me and said it had been a lovely meal.

Then she got up and stalked out.

The dialogue following that exit didn't sparkle much, but I didn't notice any loss of appetite when Daisy delivered the apple pie. It disappeared faster than snowflakes on a warm palm.

There was no more talk between Johnstone and Plant.

I corralled Plant as he left the dining room and steered him down the hall and into the parlor. He tried to pull free as we passed the lobby entrance and I gave him a friendly squeeze just above the elbow. He gasped and turned cooperative as hell. He was still rubbing his arm when he sat down on the couch after I nudged him that way.

'I don't appreciate being manhandled,' he told me.

I smiled sweetly. 'Don't kid yourself, when I manhandle you it won't be with an arm squeeze. This is just a little get-together, man to man, about a murder. Okay?'

He quit rubbing his arm, slid back on the couch and reached into his pocket for a pack of Luckies.

'What's that supposed to mean?' He was trying to be casual.

I dug out my fixings and started rolling a smoke while I explained my temporary job. He listened without expression.

'Now, that story you say you read in the paper; did it say Foote was killed or committed suicide?'

'It said something about "mysterious circumstances." *Was* it murder?'

'Yeah.'

'Who'd want to kill that old bastard? What the hell for?'

'I haven't got the foggiest. What can you tell me about the family?'

He said from what he'd heard, the Footes had been married by a justice of the peace sometime around 1909. Arthur was almost forty and Azalea was twenty. Kitty'd been born five months later.

'That was in Aberdeen?'

'The marriage, yeah. Kitty was born here. They moved right after getting married. The idea, I figure, was to keep anybody from knowing Azalea was pregnant before she was married, but it didn't work. Somehow the word got around, so Kitty was talked about and snickered at in school—'

'How'd she handle it?'

'Like a wildcat. I mean, when they made her mad she'd scream and kick and lay into anybody handy. She'd pull hair and scratch like any other girl, but she'd also use her fists and kick like a mule.'

'Where'd you hear that?'

'She told me that herself when she was living at my uncle's and I went there for Christmas, Easter and summer vacations.'

'Was she still a wildcat?'

'Not most of the time. Mostly, in fact, she seemed kind of old for her age. I suppose it was her mother and the baby being burned.'

'So you got chummy?'

'Well, sure. I mean, she was a beauty then, just like now. We got along great.'

'So what happened? I got the notion in the dining room that she's not exactly nuts about you now.'

He laughed and waved his Lucky airily.

'It was her own damned fault. She gave me all that teasing stuff, leading me on, and when I reacted like a man will, she went nuts. Tried to kill me!'

'You mean you tried to get into her pants and she fought, right?'

'Like a goddamned wildcat—and that after she'd let me mess around like crazy—'

'She tell her uncle on you?'

'Don't make me laugh. She wouldn't tattle on anybody. That girl fights her own battles and let me tell you, she fights dirty.'

'But you don't hold any grudges?'

'Why should I? Okay, so she nearly kicked me where I was hard and she bit my thumb so it bled. I belted her a few to even things up and that quieted her down.'

'And then you laid her?'

'Well, what the hell, she asked for it and believe me, she liked it. The fact is, all that fighting was just girl show—you know how that is. They grow up thinking they're not supposed to do it, let alone like it, so they make you force them and then it's not supposed to be their fault. That's their old game and you know it as well as I do.'

God knows most of us like to believe it.

'You do it with her more than once?'

'Naw. She never let me catch her alone again. But she didn't forget it. She was thinking about it when she saw who I was, don't ever think she wasn't.'

'So you figure she's still got a case on you?'

'Oh,' he said, sitting back and crossing his legs, 'I wouldn't say that. But she was remembering, just like I was.'

'What if she'd been knocked up?'

'I thought about that,' he admitted, 'but I didn't worry much. Kitty's the sort of girl who can take care of herself. She wouldn't come mewling around at me.'

I smoked my cigarette and watched him, thinking how much I'd like to punch him out. Finally I pushed that back.

'Why do you figure Azalea married a nothing guy twenty years older than her?'

He made a face and said it was because she was pregnant and he was the only fish around.

'Did your uncle know Azalea?' I asked.

He'd been sitting on the edge of the couch since he began talking about Kitty, now he slid back, narrowed his eyes and dropped his hands in his lap.

'He didn't make her pregnant, if that's what you're after.'

'Yeah? How can you be so sure?'

'I know. He wouldn't have had the nerve.'

'Was she as good-looking as Kitty?'

'Sure. Or almost. She was lots littler.'

And maybe easier to force. I asked him how come he went to stay with his uncle during vacations and not his parents? He said because he liked Aberdeen and girls there were more impressed by a guy going to school in the big city.

I asked him about his father. The subject made him solemn. He informed me, very profoundly, that his father was a very prominent evangelist. All the time Gregory had been in primary school and high school his parents were off on missionary trips to remote parts of Africa. It was plain that Gaylord, Gregory's pa, had never been very real to his son. He was a man who appeared maybe once a year, sometimes less, wearing white suits and straw hats, forever surrounded by worshiping disciples. The one year he spent in Aberdeen was as a resident preacher, but even then he was seldom home and the moment the year ended he set off on the lecture circuit, moving from coast to coast and back again, talking, talking, raising money, converting hordes.

Gregory heard him preach and was disillusioned when he discovered a library of sermons in his uncle's study that Gaylord had left. He had started reading parts of them and was stunned to find anecdotes described in Gaylord's sermons as personal experiences, all spelled out in volumes written by other men.

'I put that to him and you know what? He

gave me his saintly preacher's smile, like he was God and I was a goddamned two-year-old and told me, "All Christian experience is common. My people are no more misled than those who listen to a comedian describing experiences about what happened to him on the way to the theater."

'That,' said Gregory, 'told me all I needed to know about preachers. They're just another kind of clown.'

He slumped farther into the couch and looked ready to pout. I let him think about it for a while and then asked how well he'd known Foote.

He looked annoyed by the distraction but after a moment stirred to life and said nobody knew anything about the old fart.

'So why'd you come to the funeral?'

'That's not why I came. I just said that for Kitty's benefit. Fact is, I'm a reporter. I work for the Aberdeen *News* and I'm here to find out what happened.'

'You registered from Minneapolis.'

He waved that off. 'That was for Kitty too. I figured it'd throw her to think I was living in her town.' He leaned forward, grinning. 'Soon's I saw that story about Foote, I told my editor, hey, I knew that guy and this could be a big story since he'd come from our town. I could get a scoop. So he said okay.'

'You're getting paid for this trip?'

'Sure thing. It's my big chance.'

I didn't swallow that. Small-town newspapers I knew wouldn't pay bus fare to cover a story across town.

'I don't suppose Kitty's being here had anything to do with your wanting to cover this story?'

'Why, no,' he said with an almost straight face, 'that never occurred to me.'

I asked if his preacher pa had ever met Azalea.

He shrugged very casually. 'Could be.'

'You say he raised money. A lot of it?'

'You bet your ass. He's made a piss pile.'

'What was your mother like?'

The question confused him. It was a subject he'd never given any thought.

'Well, she's dead, you know. I guess she was like any preacher's wife. Tall, pale, delicate. Kept out of the way except when she fixed suppers or served coffee. In public Pa treated her like an angel, but at home he treated her like a retarded maid. She mostly acted like she thought he was God.'

'He still on the circuit?'

'Oh, hell, yes. He won't stop till he drops.'

I got up, thanked him for his time and stood by the door. He rose, looking disappointed. Being questioned was his idea of a good time. I wondered how he covered interviews and decided he probably tried to handle both sides of the dialogue. He finally left, saying with a smirk that he hoped he'd

95

been helpful to my investigation.

CHAPTER TEN

By ten Boswell and I had the lobby to ourselves and sat there with our smokes, staring out the windows. Small snowflakes drifted past under the streetlight, lazy and gentle.

'What do you think of the crowd we've had here the past couple days?' I asked.

He considered that awhile as he puffed on his pipe and finally said, 'Deep.'

'Yeah. Like hell's own well. There was trouble between Kitty and that Plant guy, going back a ways. Johnstone whiffed it.'

'You'd best keep a eye on that Irish fella,' he said.

'O'Keefe?'

'Uh-huh. He don't like you.'

'He's got company—but how come you say that?'

'He watches you alla time. Sneaky.'

'You figure you've found another bad guy, Boz?'

He nodded, sadly.

After a while he finished his pipe, got up and shuffled over to the window.

'It's working up,' he told me.

'You figure we're in for a pile?'

I joined him at the window. Snow was falling steady enough to make the distant streetlights fuzzy. Then, while we watched, they went from fuzzy to barely a glow and gradually disappeared.

'You'd better stay here tonight,' I said.

'Wouldn't want to be no bother.'

'No bother. You can bunk in number three, next to me.'

'Your ma won't like it.'

'She won't mind. Anyway, as long as Bertha'll feed you, you've got no problem.'

The wind came while we were still watching. All of a sudden there was nothing out there but snow so thick it was like a sheet; the lobby light reflected against it and seemed swallowed by it. We could hear the building creak and groan under the force of the wind.

I took Boswell up to three, got a towel and a blanket from the linen closet and left him sitting on the bed, pulling off his boots.

I heard something out front as I came down the stairs and reached the hall door on time to see a couple stumble in from the sidewalk and stand there, laughing and brushing off snow. At least the girl was laughing. The guy was trying to go along but didn't quite have the spirit.

The girl spotted me first, sobered at once and began apologizing for messing up the floor. I assured her it was nothing to worry about, I'd lend her a mop in the morning and

97

she could make it okay. The guy seemed to think I meant it, but the girl laughed fine and asked if I could put them up for the night. I said sure.

'Our car went into the ditch just east of town,' the girl said as he was signing in. 'We were lucky—Herb could see the town lights and we just followed the street here.'

She took off her head scarf and shook her hair loose. It was soft brown, all tucked into finger waves that hugged her small head like a cap. She had a baby nose, dimpled cheeks and Betty Boop eyes.

'It was a real adventure,' she told me. 'Herb was all grim—he said we could freeze out there, but I told him, "Uh-uh, I'm not ready yet..."'

Herb's last name was Butler. Her name, she told me, was Mary Jane. Herb signed with a deliberate hand that was waxy white with cold and his eyes watered, making his red cheeks wet. The round tip of his long nose matched his cheeks and he pulled a crumpled handkerchief from his coat pocket and dabbed at his face. The storm had scared him and he was in no mood to talk about it, but he couldn't dampen his bride's excitement.

I asked where they were headed and she said, 'Gopher Prairie,' which made Herb frown.

'Locksley,' he said. 'Gopher Prairie's in

Minnesota.'

She giggled. 'He won't admit his hometown's nowheresville. I come from another one only it's bigger.'

'Where?' I asked as I led them toward the stairs.

'Aberdeen.'

I stopped with one hand on the banister and turned to look at her.

'You know anything about a guy named Arthur Foote?'

Her big eyes got bigger.

'I don't think so—what's he do?'

'He ran a jewelry store there a few years back. I suppose it was before your time.'

'A lot was,' she assured me.

I fixed them up with a room in the south wing, not far from where I'd parked Boswell, then strolled back toward the stairs and stopped at the landing. There was a light under Kitty's door.

I paused, then strolled down the west wing hall. Johnstone's light was out, so was O'Keefe's. There was a glow under Plant's door. I walked past as far as the end apartments and came back. By then Plant's light was out too.

I returned to fourteen and tapped on the door.

'Who?' she asked after a moment.

'Carl.'

The light went out and the door opened.

'You can't stay,' she whispered as she backed up to let me in.

I asked what had gone on between her and Plant.

'It was nothing—'

'Bull. He gave you a hustle when he was home on vacation, right?'

'Of course. I was a girl and I was there. What'd you expect?'

'How'd he make out?'

'He made out.'

'Was it rape or love?'

'Neither. I didn't really want to and he made me, but I thought he was somebody special, so I didn't really fight hard.'

I figure that's the case in about nine out of ten deflowerings. The guys are always brave and the girls are scared, for obvious reasons on both sides.

'You get pregnant?'

'No.'

'Then what?'

'Then nothing. He did it the last night of his summer vacation. He was real cute, knowing I was upset that he was leaving, so I let him get so far it got to where I couldn't stop him. He promised to write but of course never did so I knew it didn't mean a thing to him. I never let him touch me again.'

'Does Johnstone know about this?'

'I suppose he's guessed it. He doesn't miss much.'

'Is he jealous?'

'He's normal.'

'So how come you let me in your room?'

'You're a cop, did I have a choice?'

'Come on, why'd you let me in the last time?'

'Well, I didn't know he was around and I'd quit him.'

'You maybe didn't know when I came in, but you did when I really got in.'

'Yeah, well, I don't always think things out, you know.'

I don't either and when I touched her and found she was only wearing a robe and it was open, we got pretty involved in something of a hurry.

'You have to be the hairiest guy I've ever touched,' she whispered later.

'That bother you?'

'Uh-uh. It's very sexy, somehow. What we ought to do, sometime, is brush each other. I'd like you to brush me. I mean, *all* my hair, you know?'

'Before of after?'

'Both.'

'That sounds like a hell of a lot of brushing.'

'Well, what are you? One of those wham-bam-thank-you-ma'am guys?'

There've been times when I didn't even say thanks, but I didn't tell her that. Anyway, that was usually when I was too drunk for

101

etiquette.

'You really like this Johnstone guy?' I asked.

'Sure. He's real nice in lots of ways. And sometimes he's funnier than hell. He gets a kick out of you, you know.'

'He'd really get a kick if he could see me now.'

She giggled and wriggled and we did it again.

CHAPTER ELEVEN

When I looked out my window in the morning I guessed we'd had at least eighteen inches of snow so far and it was still coming. I sighed, pulled on my boots, went downstairs, shrugged into my coat and headed toward the kitchen.

Bertha looked up from her coal range, which she'd been jabbing with a poker. Her broad face was apple red from the blazing coals and a strand of black hair flopped across her wide forehead.

'We're gonna need groceries,' she complained.

'Can you wait till I stoke the furnace?'

'I'm fixed till noon, but it'll probably take you longer than that to shovel a way over to Bachman's.'

The wind had swept around the back shed, leaving the door space to open, so I had no trouble getting out, but from there on the drifts were up to three feet and I floundered along, awkward as a bear with a wooden dick because the wind had made the surface hard enough to walk on in spots and then it'd give way and I'd sink to my waist. My boots filled with snow, which also blew inside my collar, and by the time I got to the west wing cellar I was about bushed. I pulled the doors open, laid them back and scrambled into the shelter below.

A few minutes later I had the fire revived, my boots emptied and my neck dry. All this took maybe twenty or thirty minutes, but it seemed like a week before I got back to the kitchen and plunked down at the kitchen table. Bertha came over with a coffeepot and when I patted her ample flank she didn't even bristle.

She poured a steaming cup of coffee for me, saying that'd ought to help and if you consider scalding your tongue a help, it did.

'That Kitty woman was out here looking for you,' she said as she put the pot back on the stove.

I leaned back and stared at her.

'Huh?'

'Your ears don't lap, you heard me.'

'What'd she want?'

'Probably more of what she got last

night—but she *said* she'd had a dream about you freezing outside and it was so real she wanted to check it out.'

'She should've stuck around—I could've froze coming back.'

'I told her there wasn't nothing could kill you and sent her to get dressed.'

'What was she wearing?'

'Not enough. You sure as hell don't waste any time, do you?'

'You're letting your imagination run away with you.'

'Don't crap me, Carl Wilcox. I know you too damned well—and I know that glow your women get. One of these days you're gonna get a dose—it's just a question of whether it'll be the clap or buckshot.'

There were steps on the stairway from the servants' quarters and then Daisy shoved the slab door open and appeared, all sleepy and shy.

Bertha asked if she was up for all day and she said she was sorry and smoothed her hair with both hands when she saw me. She had a tousled, sexy look, which annoyed Bertha, who told her to get busy slicing bread.

I left them and strolled out to the lobby, where I stood by the windows watching the snow bury Main Street. There was nobody in jail at the courthouse, so I didn't have to worry about hauling feed there, but I wondered if old Ernie had kept the fire going so the toilet wouldn't freeze. I knew Joey had to take that responsibility a lot when Ernie got sick—which usually happened when the weather turned mean.

I was thinking of calling the telephone operator to see if the world was still functioning when Kitty came down the stairs and sashayed into the lobby.

She was wearing a wool shirt and heavy sweater, both blue, and a red scarf high around her neck.

'I was worried about you,' she said.

'Nothing to worry about.'

She walked close, smelling like spring.

'I had this vivid dream that you were dead in the street out there, almost buried in the snow. Your dark hair was blowing in the wind and there was blood all over—'

'Sounds serious.'

'Don't make fun. I believe in dreams—it meant something—'

'Yeah, it meant if you don't stop cozying up to me in the open like this, you just might make it happen.'

She said, 'Oh!' and stepped back quickly.

O'Keefe came down the steps as if he'd been waiting for his cue and strolled into the lobby looking interested. If I hadn't known how the steps creaked I'd have thought he'd been hanging around up there, listening, but I knew a ghost couldn't pass over those steps without making a sound.

We exchanged grunts and then I put on my coat and went out front to fight drifts with a shovel for a while, but the snow kept coming and the wind blew everything back as fast as I could throw it away, so I backed off and went back inside.

By nine-thirty everybody'd been down for breakfast except Plant. Nobody asked about him and Ma said, no, let him sleep, when Daisy asked if she should give him a call.

I went in to see Elihu after he'd eaten. The fierce glitter was back in his eyes and he was restless. He suggested I start a walk-through tunnel from the east cellar to the west one so's I wouldn't have to hike outside to stoke the furnace over there. I told him I could shovel a hell of a lot of snow before digging a tunnel would seem like a work saver. He snorted and said I never did have any ambition except where women and drinking were concerned.

I told him about the people we had staying in the hotel and said it looked like they'd be snowed in for at least a day or so extra. That cheered him up. He asked how Daisy was doing as a waitress and I said fine. He always worried about the hired girls but never asked about Bertha. He was afraid I'd make something of it.

He told me to leave Daisy alone. She was a nice girl and he didn't want her getting all messed up with me. I told him not to worry, she was too dumb to lay down. He said that

wasn't dumb, not around me, a smart girl'd
not only stay on her feet but'd keep moving. I
had an answer for that but kept it inside
because he didn't seem like he could stand
getting too excited.

I went out to the kitchen after the visit and
saw Bertha had things all cleaned up and
cleared off. She didn't ask about Elihu. She
said that man Plant still hadn't come down
for breakfast and she, by God, wasn't going
to fix one when he did.

I said fine.

She asked when the hell I was going for
groceries. I said give me your list. She sat
down and started writing.

'Elihu's looking mean again,' I said.

'Oh?'

That was real casual. She kept on writing.

'He eat his breakfast?' I asked.

'Every crumb.'

Very satisfied.

'He's worried about Daisy.'

She stopped writing and squinted at me.

'He's afraid you're ragging her too much.'

She snorted and waggled the pencil.
'You're a goddamned liar, Carl Wilcox.'

'Come on, you know blamed well we can't
keep a girl here morn'n a few weeks because
you rag 'em so hard.'

'It ain't me that drives them off—it's *her*.'

Her was Ma.

'You make a great team,' I said.

107

She got up, handed me her list and shooed me out.

I waded across the street towing a sled my nephew, Hank, had abandoned some years back. It was a relief but no real surprise to find Ed Bachman sitting on a stool behind the cash register. He was the oldest son of Charley Bachman, who'd started the store some twenty years before and now rarely showed up. Ed was at least fifty, but everybody still called him Sonny.

'When'd you take up chewing tobacco?' I asked, looking at the wad in his cheek.

He looked sheepish and said it was a prune.

I handed him Bertha's list, which brightened him a little but didn't make him blinding. He took a folding box from under the counter, opened it and started moving around, filling it. I went and perched on his stool.

The telephone rang. I picked it up and said hello.

'You don't sound like Sonny,' accused a lady.

'That's not surprising,' I said, 'since I'm not him.'

'Well, who are you?'

I told her. She had to think that over a little.

'Where's Sonny?'

'Getting my groceries.'

'And he's left you sitting there beside the

108

cash register?'

'It's pretty safe,' I assured her. 'You can't open it without making the bell ring.'

There was another thoughtful silence and then she asked me to ask Sonny if she could get some groceries delivered. 'This is Mrs. Syvertson,' she added significantly.

'You delivering groceries today?' I yelled at Sonny.

He said no. I passed that on.

'Tell him who's calling,' she said.

I did.

He put down my half-filled box of groceries and came over to take the telephone.

His voice was totally without sarcasm or condescension as he explained that it was snowing out. I'd have been impressed except I knew the man didn't have the capacity for either attitude. Apparently Mrs. Syvertson knew it too because she didn't get mad. After a while Sonny hung up and went back to my groceries.

I told him she'd not be in his store to shop when spring came back. He said that was okay, she never had anyway.

My box was about full when Puck came in the door. He was bundled up till he looked like a ball of rags and it took several minutes for him to unwrap enough to breathe with comfort.

I asked how he was getting along with Abigail and he said just dandy. When Sonny came to greet him he handed over a list that I could see had been written by the old maid.

'Looks like you two have hit it off just fine,' I said.

'Why not? She can cook and I can haul.'

'Nobody'd ask for more at your age. Didn't your folks come from Aberdeen?'

'First from New York State.'

'To Aberdeen.'

'Close,' he said and grinned. He was missing two lower front teeth lost long ago in a hockey game. He'd spit them out and played two more periods.

'Ever know a guy there named Gregory Plant?'

'He play hockey?'

'I doubt it.'

'Well, lots of guys from there didn't. Who I remember is old Harlan Bowman. Played for Notre Dame. We never played against them—I just heard about him from somebody.'

'You make more sense when you're on the sauce,' I told him.

'I suppose so. But I hadda give it up. Abigail won't allow it. She give me fair notice.'

'You know,' I said, 'the more you talk the more I think I should lock you up on suspicion.'

'Of what?' he bristled.

'If I could think of what, I'd do it.'

I hauled my box of groceries out to the sled, lashed it down with twine loaned by Sonny and waded back to the hotel. The plow hadn't even made a pass at the highway yet.

When I got the box into the kitchen and Bertha had gone through everything she started getting red. She turned to me, fat arms akimbo, and demanded to know where the hell they were.

'What?'

'You *know* what.'

'If anything's missing it's because you left it off the list. Sonny wouldn't leave anything out.'

'I give you fifty cents for my candy bars, now where are they?'

I managed to look horrified and she reached for me. I slipped under her arm, but she grabbed my coat as I scooted by. Luckily I'd unbuttoned it when I first came in or she'd have jerked me silly—as it was she just peeled the coat off. I reached the open space by the doors leading to the dining room and turned around to watch her go through the coat pockets and pull out ten candy bars, which she lined up deliberately on the table.

'Oh, *that*'s what you meant. I thought I'd forgot something important, like cornstarch.'

'What you'd best do,' she told me as she sat down by the candy bars, 'is go see if that fellow Plant's got out of bed yet. The way you handle the fires he could've frozen to death.'

111

I went back to the lobby and looked in. Mary Jane was sitting in a rocker next to O'Keefe, who was telling her a cock-and-bull story about when he was a cop. Herb, her husband, sat across the room with his back to Main Street, looking bored. His wife was smiling, all bright-eyed and excited because she knew she was having an adventure.

I climbed the stairs and drifted west to nineteen. There were no sounds inside, so after a few seconds of listening I tapped on the door.

'Plant!' I called.

Nothing.

I knocked harder.

More nothing.

I opened the door and peered in.

The green shades were drawn, but enough light came through to show me the bed was empty. I stepped inside and looked around. There are no closets in the Wilcox Hotel; guests leave most of their stuff in their suitcases, the few things they hang up they suspend on hooks along the wall behind the door where Ma has left hangers. There were no clothes hung up and no suitcase on the stand at the foot of the bed. I opened the commode and found he hadn't used it.

Except for the wrinkled sheets and thrown-back blankets, there was no sign that anyone had ever been in the room. I raised the window shades and looked out on the snow-covered balcony. Nothing but drifting snow. No tracks, no unusual lumps.

There was nothing but dust under the bed and little of that.

O'Keefe was still telling Mary Jane what a fascinating guy he was when I got back to the lobby. I sat down next to Herb and leaned close.

'How long you been down here?' I asked.

He glanced wearily at his watch and said about half an hour or so.

'You see a tall galoot in a gray suit come down with his suitcase?'

'No. Where'd anybody go? We couldn't even hire somebody to go pull our car out.'

I got up, went over and glanced at the register and then headed for Elihu's room.

The old man was dozing. Ma sat near the window, working her needle on a quilt spread over her knees.

'You didn't check out the Plant guy, did you?' I asked.

Her head jerked up.

'What's the matter—he skip?'

'His room's empty. No suitcase, nothing. Nobody saw him leave that I know of.'

'I thought he had that sly look last night—'

'So did I, but I didn't think it had anything to do with him planning to beat the bill. He couldn't go anyplace—the roads are all snowed in.'

'Mebbe he didn't have sense enough to

113

know it. He might've tried...'

I went back upstairs, walked past nineteen, up the three steps to the extreme west wing apartments and into the one that was empty, a two-room affair consisting of a bedroom and a kitchen facing south. The wooden fire escape was outside the kitchen window and I looked the platform over but couldn't tell whether it'd been used. The way the snow was coming down and blowing, tracks would have disappeared within half an hour.

When I got back to the lobby nearly the whole crowd was there. Johnstone was in Elihu's swivel chair by the window, glaring at the snowfall, Mary Jane and Herb Butler were standing close together by the gumball machine next to the newspaper table under the wall clock. He was handing her a gumball while they both stared at me. It was a white one. Boswell was still parked in the rocker nearest the registration cove and had his stinking pipe going full steam. Kitty, seated at the salesman's desk, looked up from a letter she was writing and Buff stared at me from the rocker near the front door.

'Where's O'Keefe?' I asked Johnstone.

'Went to get me some cigars.'

The telephone rang and I made a move that way, but Ma beat me to it. I turned back to Johnstone.

'How long ago'd O'Keefe leave?'

He shrugged. 'A little while before you

114

came down.'

Ma came and told me Syvertson was on the phone.

'I've been talking with Joey,' the mayor said. 'He's got laryngitis—can't hardly make a sound—listen—we've got to get someone in here to work on this murder—'

'You gave up suicide?'

'Well, we have to be thorough—'

'Fine. Who do you want to bring in, the FBI or maybe Scotland Yard?'

'This is no joking matter.'

'Okay. But right now we got a blizzard, in case you hadn't noticed and besides that there's a new problem. A guest who showed up last night has disappeared.'

He wanted to know all about that and I ran through it for him. I'd just finished when Carrie, the substitute operator, broke in and said she had an important message for me. There was trouble at the pool hall and I was wanted right now.

I told Syvertson I'd talk to him later, hung up, grabbed my coat and charged into the blizzard. The driving snow blinded me but was so deep I couldn't move fast enough to do any damage if I ran into anything, so I slogged along with both hands in front and cut what I hoped was a straight path across streets toward the pool hall. Pretty quick I came up against a building, recognized the step up as the hardware store entrance and

115

stumbled two doors beyond to the one I was after and went busting in.

'Hurry,' yelled Ole, the bartender, 'they're just about to go at it.'

I brushed past him, trotted the length of the beer bar while pulling off my mitts and entered the back room.

Three guys were facing the southeast corner where Jack O'Keefe stood in a crouch, holding a cue with both hands and waving it easy before him. The men with their backs to me also had cues, but nobody looked interested in pool. O'Keefe's teeth were bared in a wolfish grin as his beady eyes swung back and forth between the men confronting him.

I jerked a cue from the nearest rack and jabbed its heavy end into the right kidney of the tallest man. He jumped and snapped his head around.

'Drop it, Packard. You guys do the same.'

Packard started a quick turn and as he came around I smacked his knuckles with the cue butt. He swore and dropped his weapon, which clattered on the floor. His two sidekicks moved away from him and put their cues on the nearest table. They looked relieved.

'This son of a bitch clubbed Puck,' yelled Packard. 'He's there on the floor. Look at 'im!'

'Yeah. He's breathing. O'Keefe, put your cue on the table.'

116

He came out of his crouch, still grinning, but made no move to mind.

'Then what?' he asked.

'We'll sort out what happened here.' I turned my head without taking my eyes from O'Keefe and told Ole to call Doc. He said he already had.

'I'll tell you what happened here,' said O'Keefe. 'This punchy hick,' he nodded toward Puck, 'got sore 'cause I was beating his ass in pool and took a pass at me. I decked him. Then these other morons tried to jump me.'

'Okay,' I said. 'Now put the cue down.'

'You still got yours.'

'That's right, but I'm the cop. I get to keep mine.'

He leaned his cue against the wall within easy reach.

I turned to Packard and asked for his version.

He said there'd been nasties between Puck and this son of a bitch from the first break and then some name calling and when Puck offered to knock O'Keefe's block off the son of a bitch had told him no wonder he couldn't shoot straight, he was using a crooked cue and when Puck stopped to sight along it, O'Keefe hauled off and coldcocked him.

The other players backed him up and Ole, who probably had been back at the bar where he couldn't see a thing, swore it was just the

117

way they said.

I glanced at O'Keefe, who was starting to lean toward his stashed cue.

'Get your coat,' I told him. 'We're going for a walk.'

'Where to?'

'City Hall.'

'My room's at the hotel.'

'Not tonight.'

He reached for his cue.

I shoved past him with mine and knocked it to the floor. He grabbed my stick with both hands and gave a hell of a yank. I let go, his elbow slammed into the wall and pain froze him for half a second. I yanked his jacket down to his elbows, spun him around, applied a hammerlock with one hand and grabbed the seat of his britches with the other and pulled so tight his balls were in a vise. Then I frog-marched him out past the bar. Ole happily ran to open the front door and out we went into the snow. The three pool players kept us company for about twenty feet, hooting it up, but only Packard stuck with me to open the City Hall door. I marched O'Keefe back to the cell, shoved him in and turned the lock. He stumbled over to the bunk, wheeled, sat and glared at me.

Packard wanted to keep crowing, but I hustled him out and returned to the Irishman.

'That was a dumb play,' I told him. 'If I

hadn't hauled you out of there they'd have beaten your brains out. Nobody's good enough to whip three guys without a tommy gun. I could've stood and watched them do the job and nobody in town would've faulted me and no jury in the state would've given them so much as a hickey if they'd killed you. Now tomorrow we'll see the judge and if there's any damages you'll pay. That'll be it if Puck's not hurt bad, which isn't likely since he's got a head like a bowling ball. Your biggest worry is how sore Johnstone's gonna be that you didn't just buy his cigars and bring 'em back.'

He didn't thank me for my kindness, but some of the fire went out of his eyes.

'You made me look bad.' That wasn't a complaint, it was a threat.

'Don't worry about it—nobody in Minneapolis'll ever know. Listen. Did you hear anything unusual at the hotel last night after you'd gone to your room?'

He shook his head.

'You know what room Plant was in?'

He reached into his shirt pocket for cigarettes, pulled one from the pack and squinted at me.

'Yeah. Next to mine.'

'You hear him in there?'

He shook his head, started to light up and found his matchbook empty.

'Got a light?' he asked.

119

'Sure.'

He came to the barred door and halted.

'Put the cigarette in your mouth, your hands behind your back and your head against the bars,' I said.

For a second he considered telling me to go to hell, but he wanted the light and finally obeyed. I lit his cigarette and he went back and sat down.

'I've been in this cell a few times myself,' I told him. 'Been in lots of them. Everything you're thinking about trying to pull, I've thought about too.'

He looked bored and asked what'd happened to Plant.

I told him.

'You look in Kitty's room?' he asked.

'You think they're cozy?'

'Hell, you could see from his shit-eating grin last night that he'd had her. Probably got it again.'

I went over to Doc's and learned that Puck was okay and had gone home to Abigail's.

I hiked over to check him out for myself. It was only a couple blocks, but what with drifts, flying snow and cutting wind it seemed like a couple miles.

Abigail didn't want to let me in, but Puck convinced her it was safe with him around and we went into the living room, which was right of the entry and she retreated to her room on the left.

I asked what had caused the ruckus.

He chuckled and said he'd been trying to explain it to Abigail and it wasn't easy. There was just something about O'Keefe that got your back up the minute he showed. He never said it out, but he let everybody know he thought they were dumb hicks. He wore his contempt like a red derby. During the first game O'Keefe didn't show any particular savvy and lost. They played another round and he lost again and looked sour and said why not make it worth trying with a little bet? Puck, who hadn't been straining himself any to look good, agreed. Puck won the next one too and agreed to double the bet and, of course, from then on, everything O'Keefe touched dropped.

'I mean,' Puck told me, 'that son of a bitch couldn't have missed if he'd been shooting with a hoe handle. I told him he was a goddamned hustler and he told me I should take a good look at me cue and when I did I came to with a headache. He must be damned near as fast as you, Carl.'

I said I hoped not since I didn't have anything else going for me.

'Uh-huh. Well, I'll tell you, that's one mean bastard. Hell, he had no call to hit me like that.'

I asked if he were willing to press charges and he just snorted.

Back in Joey's office at City Hall I thought

for a while as I warmed up, put my coat back on, went out into the blowing snow, made a sharp turn at the corner of City Hall, walked the narrow space between it and the hotel and stopped near the bottom of the wooden fire escape.

The howling north wind had swept the walk clean and piled snow in a lovely, smooth drift around the ladder bottom. I took a couple steps into the drift and was in over my boot tops. I took another step and felt something between my boot and the frozen ground. About five minutes of pawing through snow uncovered enough of the body to identify Gregory Plant. A little more kicking around located the suitcase.

I squatted a few seconds, looking around. The snow was still falling hard and fast enough to screen the body and me from anyone in the hotel or anywhere else over ten feet away.

Back in the office I telephoned Doc.

He wasn't grateful but agreed to come.

I thought of calling Syvertson but didn't feel up to it and rolled a smoke, which I'd about finished when Doc showed up looking grumpy.

I told him where the body was.

He shook his head. 'I thought it was bad examining Foote in a drafty shed at seventeen below. Now you want me to examine a body in a blizzard. How're you going to top that?'

'Maybe I can find one on top of the water tower during a tornado. You want to quit bitching and do your job?'

Eventually we got the frozen body over to the hotel shed, where I perched it on two boards supported by sawhorses.

Plant had been dumped off the fire escape platform, stark naked with his hands and feet tied and a gag in his mouth. Doc couldn't find any damage other than that caused by the fall and ventured to guess he'd hit the ground alive.

'Of course, he wouldn't have lasted long after that. It's also possible he strangled on his vomit because of the gag.'

'We got a killer who's not exactly tenderhearted, right?'

'Vicious. Have you advised the mayor of this yet?'

'No. I wanted to be sure we had a corpse first.'

'That,' said Doc, 'I will swear to. I might even go so far as to aver this was not suicide.'

'Aver? Is that anything like saying you're positive?'

'It is.'

'Doc, you're the only guy I know whose big words are short. Sometimes I think Corden doesn't deserve you.'

'Yes,' he said. 'Go call the mayor.'

CHAPTER TWELVE

People were heading for the dining room and lunch as I went down the hall to call Syvertson, who complained at once that I was keeping him from the table. My news made him forget food in a hurry; he said he'd be right over. He was so upset I tried to make it a little easier by reminding him the victim wasn't a Cordenite and never had been. That helped. He said he'd be with me as soon as he'd had lunch.

Folks had vacated the dining room by the time he bustled in and he suggested we conduct the interrogations in the dining room booth nearest the kitchen.

'We'll sit them across from us and cross-question them, you know?'

I reminded him that mayors didn't usually take on the business of questioning witnesses or conducting police investigations in general.

He explained very patiently that since I was new on the job and there was no one else around in a position of authority he had a duty to become totally involved.

'It's important for the citizens of the community to know their authorities have matters under complete control.'

I admitted I hadn't ever thought about things quite that way and he assured me that was no great fault, it was just because I'd never accepted any responsibilities in my life while he had done little else. Then he suggested we open the questioning with Kitty.

'Is that because you figure she's the best suspect or the best looking?'

That brought on a lecture about the folly of frivolity in serious situations and I surrendered and went after the lady.

Kitty's face had an almost starched look and even her usual fluid walk was a mite stiff as we entered the dining room. Syvertson stood up, made a move as if he were going to bow but only nodded his head and waved her grandly into the booth. Then he slid in across from her, rested both elbows on the table and leaned forward. He apologized for having to put her through this when she was still grieving for her lost father and explained tediously why it was necessary.

She nodded, still without expression.

He asked how well she had known Plant. Her dark eyes flickered my way and returned to him. She gave him the bare bones of the relationship without mentioning the semirape.

'You were never intimate?' he asked.

She studied him for a moment, trying to guess how much he knew. Finally she took a slow, deep breath and said, 'We weren't lovers, if that's what you're getting at.'

'Well, uh, yes. Thank you.' He turned to me with a questioning look.

'Did Johnstone think you'd been cozy with Plant?' I asked.

'He didn't have any reason to.'

'He might've thought he did from your reaction last night.'

Syvertson's head turned as he tried to take us both in and he leaned more toward Kitty.

'What's the relationship between this Mr. Johnstone and you?'

She folded her slender hands on the table and said, 'I used to work for him.'

'His secretary?'

'Sort of.'

He stared into her eyes a few seconds, overlooking the long-nailed fingers almost under his nose, and asked how come, if she no longer worked for the man, he was here in Corden?

'Maybe he likes funerals. Why don't you ask him?'

He drew back a little and said he would. Her spikiness had hurt him; he'd hoped to charm her and obviously he hadn't.

'How'd you feel when you heard Plant had been murdered?'

'I was scared,' she said and the admission seemed to surprise her. 'Then I just felt sort of numb.' She glanced at me. 'You know, I realized then I didn't really hate him. Back when we knew each other and he treated me

126

bad, he was just a stupid kid, and so was I. And from what I saw last night, I didn't think he'd grown up or got any smarter. But he sure didn't deserve what happened. I can't understand why anybody'd be crazy enough to kill him, let alone Arthur. I mean, that's really spooky...'

We sat in silence for several seconds and finally I asked her how well her brother Buff had known Plant.

She slumped back on the bench and shook her head.

'He didn't know him at all. There must've been ten years' difference in their ages and just about no contact.'

After a few more questions Syvertson reluctantly decided we weren't going anywhere, thanked her for her cooperation and escorted her back to the lobby.

He came back with Buff in tow.

Buff confirmed that he hadn't known Plant. Syvertson asked him what his sister thought of Plant and he said it would be whatever she had told him and if he thought she'd killed Plant he must be crazy because she was nowhere near big enough to do the job. Syvertson got mad and said maybe not but Buff probably was.

'Like hell, he was half again as big as me,' sneered Buff.

Syvertson gave me a significant glance and said a man didn't have to be big to be dangerous.

'Which reminds me,' he said, 'what was that trouble over at the pool hall about?'

'O'Keefe and Puck tangled. Puck got flattened and I tossed O'Keefe in the pokey.'

'Well! You might've told me this before. It sounds to me like this fellow O'Keefe is the one we should be questioning.'

'I already did. He claims he didn't see or hear anything and never saw Plant before last night.'

He scowled over that and then asked if O'Keefe had given me any trouble when I arrested him.

'I'd have expected a man like that to resist.'

'I reasoned with him.'

Syvertson looked back at Buff, who was grinning broadly. That offended the mayor and he sat up straight and glared.

'Why was this fellow Plant here?'

Buff spread his hands and said, 'Don't ask me. He *said* he came for the funeral.'

'He came too late.'

'Yeah. Is that a crime?'

'I'll thank you not to get sarcastic with me, young man. It seems to me I heard you're in the navy. Why aren't you in uniform?'

'You don't have to wear it when you're on liberty.'

Syvertson turned to me. 'Is that right? I never saw a navy man out of uniform before—'

'So how'd you know the guy was a gob if he wasn't in his monkey suit?'

He thought that over, absorbed it and scowled at Buff again.

'All right. We'll talk to you again. When you go back to the lobby, send that fellow Johnstone back.'

'Yes, *sir*,' said Buff with a mocking salute and off he went.

'A smart aleck,' said Syvertson. 'I thought they taught respect for authority in the navy.'

'Some take more teaching than others.'

He grunted and as Johnstone came through the dining entrance leaned my way and said I should question this fellow.

Johnstone sat down, took a cigar from his inside coat pocket and began unwrapping it. The mayor promptly forgot he'd asked me to do the questioning and wanted to know how come Johnstone had cigars if he'd sent his man to buy a supply?

'I don't wait till I'm out of gas to fill the tank' was his answer.

'Prudent,' conceded Syvertson, and he sat back on the bench.

I asked if Johnstone had heard any unusual sounds during the night and he said he had not. He got up once to go to the bathroom. There was no one else moving around and he heard nothing but the wind blowing and the hotel freezing.

I asked if he'd known Gregory Plant's

129

uncle. He said he'd heard of him but they never met. He had met Gregory's father. I asked how come.

'Kitty wanted to see him,' he said. 'We went to one of his meetings when he was in Minneapolis. He was something.'

Syvertson came to life.

'Was that Gaylord Plant—the evangelist?'

'Nobody else. The old stem-winder himself. The man who gathers things of this world by promising folks everything in the next one.'

'He's on radio,' said Syvertson.

'Every Sunday.' He grinned at me. 'You probably never heard him, but it's worth a couple hours. You know, most of those born-again boys start off nice and quiet and build up to the hysteria, but he starts right off at the peak and never comes down. Fantastic showman.'

'He has a powerful message,' said the mayor.

'Yeah, you give, I'll take. Greatest message in the world.'

'You don't respect him.'

'Respect doesn't half touch it. I'm awed.'

'How long's he been doing this?' I asked.

'Oh, fifteen, maybe twenty years. He started out in Aberdeen, went big in South Dakota, moved on to the Twin Cities, then east and finally took over California.'

That figured.

130

The three of us were silent until I asked Johnstone if he'd known Gregory Plant. He said no, he'd never seen him before he showed up at the hotel.

'Kitty ever talk about him?'

'No. Why would she?'

'Because he raped her a few years back, when she was living at his uncle's place.'

His smile disappeared.

'She never told me anything like that. Where'd you hear it?'

'From her. Does it interest you?'

He shrugged casually but scowled murder.

Syvertson demanded to know why I'd asked that question?

'To get the answer,' I told him. 'You want to take over now?'

'You're implying that Kitty and this fellow—'

'I'm not implying a damned thing. He came here because of her. They're old friends.'

Syvertson gaped at him.

'You're old enough to be her father!'

'Yeah, so are you. But I saw you giving her the eye when you brought her back to the lobby.'

Syvertson sank back, dropping his hands in his lap. A thought came to him and he turned to me.

'She's not a secretary at all, is she? She's a kept woman.'

Johnstone grinned. 'Nobody keeps Kitty,' he said. 'I give her things now and then. She doesn't do a thing she doesn't want to.'

'If you knew before now that Gregory'd raped Kitty, what would you have done?' I asked.

'Probably break his neck.'

'You? Or would you have O'Keefe handle it?'

'That's a job I'd save for myself.'

'The job's already done. He was murdered last night.'

Johnstone's eyes opened wide. He glanced at the mayor and shook his head. 'If I'd known that, I wouldn't have said what I did.'

Syvertson, who'd been getting more and more twitchy, leaned forward and asked what sort of business Johnstone was in.

'I buy and sell things.'

'Goods, property—what?'

'What's this got to do with murder?'

The mayor turned red and I butted in.

'The mayor peddles some real estate himself. He'd like to find out how a man like you gets rich at it.'

'That's simple. Do business with people not as smart as you are.'

Obviously Syvertson was never going to get rich in real estate. I brought Johnstone back to Kitty, asking if she'd ever talked about Foote.

'We didn't talk about her old man much.'

'You never knew what he did for a living?'

'She said he was a jeweler once. I guess I figured he was retired or something. It was none of my business.'

'How about the mother, Azalea? Not much talk about her either?'

'Yeah, she mentioned her now and then. Liked her. We didn't go on about family.'

'What did you talk about?'

'None of your goddamned business.'

'Was she interested in your business?'

'She listened when I talked about it, yeah. I never figured she was studying to be a real estate agent.'

'She ever see any other men?'

'I don't know. Never asked. Didn't want to hear.'

'How come you showed up here for the funeral?'

'It seemed like the right thing to do. Let her know I was interested.'

'You didn't maybe think she was taking a walk, did you?'

He looked past me, closed his eyes for a moment and managed to look embarrassed.

'Kitty's moody,' he said at last. 'Impulsive. We had some good times and some bad. I've tried to be around when I thought I could help and she appreciates that. We understand each other, whatever happens.'

I felt he wanted us to believe that almost as badly as he wanted to believe it himself. Then

133

his expression turned angry.

'Look, you're not getting anywhere. How about we quit now?'

I looked at Syvertson, who nodded.

'Send Butler back, will you?' I asked as Johnstone got up.

'Why'd he get mad?' Syvertson asked me after Johnstone left.

'He gave away how he felt about Kitty.'

'You think he did it—or had that fellow O'Keefe do it?'

'Who knows? I suspect he never had a reason before he came in here just now. I don't think he was lying when he said Kitty never told about Plant. It's not the kind of thing she'd tell a guy like him.'

'She's a strange girl.'

'Yeah, aren't they all.'

Butler was a born suspect. He sat down across from us with the hangdog, guilty look of a man who'd spent his life not measuring up to his superior's expectations. From the moment the mayor began asking questions, Butler had to paw them over, looking for tricks and traps in every word. When the mayor asked if he'd ever met any of the hotel guests before his arrival the night before, he insisted that they all be listed before he'd answer and even then qualified his answers, saying they were according to the best of his knowledge.

He said he'd heard strange popping sounds

134

in the night and people in the halls. It was possible that two persons had gone past his door. He had heard no talking.

Syvertson asked how come he was in Corden, and he explained that he and his wife were returning to Huron from a honeymoon trip to Fargo and had been stopped by the storm.

'Fargo? For a honeymoon?'

'Well, that's where Mary Jane's aunt lives. Aunt Linia's husband is a very successful dentist there and she's got money of her own and paid for a hotel room downtown where we stayed. Aunt Linia's crazy about Mary Jane and wanted to get acquainted with me, so that's why she made the offer—'

Syvertson looked bewildered. 'How come they didn't have you stay in their house if they're so successful?'

'Well, with us being just married and all they thought it'd be better for us to be by ourselves but still in town so we could come around for dinner and visits.'

I asked what kind of a job be was going to in Huron.

'I'm an accountant in the First National Bank there. And I do part-time work for a clothing store and the druggist.'

'You know any bankers in Aberdeen?'

He shook his head.

'Where'd you meet your wife?'

'In Huron. She has an account in our

bank.'

'She born there?'

'Uh—no, I don't think so.'

'You don't know?' demanded Syvertson.

'Well, Mary Jane doesn't talk about the past. She wants to talk about where we're going.'

'Where's that?' I asked.

'Up,' he said and didn't smile.

We stared at him and finally the mayor said, 'You mean heaven?'

'Oh, no, not for a while yet. No, Mary Jane wants us to move to a bigger town. Like Sioux Falls or even Minneapolis. Somewhere with greater opportunities for advancement.'

I figured for real advancement she'd have to pick another husband. We talked a little more and then said thanks and asked him to send his wife back when he went to the lobby.

'I think I'd ought to be here when you talk to her,' he said.

I stared at him and he shifted his eyes.

'You think we're going to make a pass at her?' I asked.

He squared his bony shoulders.

'She might be afraid. She's just a girl, you know.'

'She's old enough to be married,' said Syvertson, 'and she doesn't strike me as a nervous Nellie, so you just send her in and she'll be fine.'

Butler's stubborn look slowly caved in and

he rose in resignation and drooped back to the lobby.

Mary Jane bounced in, full of excited anticipation.

'Where were you born?' I asked as she settled down with a flurry in front of us.

'Golly, you going to get my whole history?'

'Probably not. You want to answer the question?'

'Sure. In a bitty town west of Huron. My mother was taken there for the delivery because Daddy knew the doctor—actually I think he was a first cousin—and there was a blizzard just like now—maybe worse—and I was born at three-fifteen A.M. and the next year there was a fire in the little town and nobody lives there anymore.'

Syvertson beamed at her and she beamed back with her deep-brown eyes all aglow under black lashes. She had heavy, dark eyebrows, apple cheeks, dimples and a smile white enough to light a dungeon.

I asked if she knew any of the people staying in the hotel.

'No, but I'm getting acquainted. I think old Boswell's just precious—you think he might be Santa Claus? And that Mr. Johnstone is so distinguished looking and Jack's a terribly interesting man—'

'What makes him interesting?' I asked.

'Well, he's done just about everything. He used to be a policeman, you know, and he's

137

worked as a union organizer—been in awful fights and things. I never met a person who even knew somebody from a union before.'

'They're scarce in these parts,' I allowed.

'And Mr. Johnstone's rich.'

She said that like she thought we should all cross ourselves.

'Did he tell you that?'

'Jack did. He says Mr. Johnstone can buy anything he wants. I asked him, just to tease, you know, "How about eternal life?" And he said, "Who wants it?" Can you imagine?'

'Just about. You ever been to Aberdeen?'

'I've never been much of anywhere before now. Fargo's a goofy place for a honeymoon, huh? But Hubby was all for it because it wouldn't cost us anything and he wanted to get on the good side of Aunt Linia. I wish she lived in the South. Why doesn't anybody have relatives in the South, where it's warm?'

I said that was too deep for me and asked if she'd heard any sounds in the night.

Lord, no, she went to sleep the minute her head hit the pillow and nothing but eight hours of sleep would wake her. That made me think her honeymoon must have been overworked early or, worse, had never amounted to anything. Considering Butler, it seemed more likely she'd have been as well off sleeping as trying to get any thrills from him. He'd probably be afraid strenuous activity would give him an expensive appetite.

138

When she finally whisked off, Syvertson smiled indulgently and said what a lovely child and an ideal couple. I thought they'd probably do fine if you could shrink them down for a wedding cake decoration.

Our last customer was Boswell. He hadn't heard or seen anything, just slept. Said he could tell us about a dream he had if we were interested and Syvertson wasn't, so I said I'd let it pass.

We walked back to the lobby and Johnstone met me at the door and wanted to know when I was going to talk with O'Keefe. I said I already had.

'Where?'

'He got himself into a little ruckus with the natives. I had to put him in protective custody. Does he get into trouble often?'

'Certainly not. Oh, he rubs some people the wrong way now and then—but he can take care of himself. What happened?'

'He coldcocked a local hero with his cue at the pool hall.'

That didn't surprise him enough to show, but he wanted to know where his man was. I said he was in jail.

This time he didn't even try to hide his surprise.

'You must've had a lot of help.'

'The bartender held the door for me.'

His eyes narrowed. 'I want to see him. Now.'

'Get your coat.'

O'Keefe was dozing like a bored cat as we approached the cell but woke and was on his feet by the time we stopped in front of the bars.

'You okay?' asked Johnstone.

'I been better.'

'How the hell'd he get you in here?'

'Ahh!'

Johnstone looked at me accusingly and back at his man.

'He hasn't even got a gun.'

O'Keefe shrugged. 'The place was full of his pals.'

Johnstone peered at him and shook his head.

'I don't see that they marked you any.'

O'Keefe shrugged again.

Johnstone stared at him a few seconds longer, then turned to me.

'What's the charge?'

'Assault, disturbing the peace, resisting an officer—maybe a few more if you'd like.'

'I want him out of there.'

'You afraid of something?'

'Who do I talk to? A judge, right? I want to see the judge.'

The judge was at dinner and not exactly tickled pink about having it interrupted, but he was a gentleman about it. He came into the parlor where his maid had left us and absentmindedly carried his napkin along. He

140

didn't offer to shake hands, so it didn't get in his way.

I told him what'd happened without mentioning the attempt at resistance or my technique for delivering him to the jail.

'You say Puck won't press charges?' he asked.

I nodded.

'What about damages?'

'Nothing to mention.'

The judge looked at Johnstone, pricing the fancy suit and the fine silver hair and I waited to see whether envy or respect would take charge.

'This O'Keefe man works for you, is that it?'

'He does.'

'You'll be accountable for him.'

'Certainly.'

'Very well.' He turned to me. 'Release the man. Have him at my chambers tomorrow at eleven A.M., sharp. Good evening.'

We slogged back to City Hall, where I unlocked the prisoner and told him the feed bag was on at the hotel. I didn't get any thanks, but he said he'd remember me. I didn't figure that meant he'd be sending me a Christmas card.

CHAPTER THIRTEEN

After dinner everybody went to the movies but Ma, Boswell, Elihu and me.

I went in to talk with Elihu.

He was propped up by four pillows and his mussed white hair floated around his skull like a thin cloud. His eyes had recovered their mad-hawk look.

'I thought I went out to the kitchen,' he told me hoarsely. 'There was something out there tearing up the floor. I couldn't see what it was, but it made a hell of a racket and when I hollered stop, everything got still as death. It was awful. Then a voice like God's told me to back out and I did. It isn't really happening, is it?'

I assured him the floor was still intact.

'Don't be too sure. You didn't hear that voice. I never heard nothing more awful. It meant something—sounded like God but it could've been the devil maybe.'

I said I guessed they had a lot in common.

He gave me a frown but after a second's thought, got a wicked grin and then he chuckled. His wild eyes strayed around, taking in the shadows beyond the lamplight beside his bed and his expression grew confused.

'I dunno what's happening, you know? I

can look up at the ceiling and see pictures that move. I looked this afternoon and there was this fella in a rowboat with a hairy dog. Fella was fishing. Caught a bluegill. I could see it flip and the water fly from its tail and the sun catching the drops so they sparkled and the dog barked, all excited. I couldn't hear him, but I could see his mouth open and his head bob. Ain't that something when you look at the ceiling and see moving pictures? And there are ghosts out tearing up your kitchen. None of it makes sense. I know something's happening, something awful, but it don't make sense. None of it.'

'Not much ever does.'

'It used to. I remember when it did but I don't remember too good. I just know it did for a fact.'

'Not in my lifetime.'

'Where's your ma?' he asked.

'Probably working on tomorrow's menu with Bertha.'

'She's always off somewheres. Only hangs around when she thinks I'm asleep.'

'Well, that's most of the time.'

'A piss ant lot you know. Been awake plenty. Can't sort things out, so I keep quiet. Something's happening, though. I can feel it. Something awful.'

'You'll be okay.'

'The hell I will. Everything's going to hell, you know—'

'You've been saying that for sixty years.'

'I been right for sixty years. Only now it's going faster. I know when it began—'

He broke off as Ma came in and right away he started griping about when he was going to get supper. She was trying to explain to him that he'd already eaten as I slipped out through the French doors to the parlor off the bedroom. A little later she joined me where I sat by the window looking out at the snow.

'What'll you do if he dies?' I asked.

She sat down in the upholstered chair across from me, turned on the lamp, picked up a quilt square from the side table and began stabbing it with her needle.

'I'll get an apartment in Aquatown. Visit Minneapolis. Maybe go to California and see Aunt Leck.'

'Sell the hotel?'

'If you won't run it, yes.'

'Sounds like you're looking forward to it.'

'That's how I manage,' she said, without a pause in her stitching. 'I try to think of what good can come from anything that happens. If I get sick, I'll read. If I go blind, I'll listen to the radio. When everything else is gone, I'll make do with God alone.'

I thought, God help God when it comes to that.

We could hear our guests in the lobby and pretty soon Ma set her sewing aside and said we should go out and see to their

144

entertainment. I said my buck-and-wing was a little rusty and got a glance that told me she wouldn't tolerate obscenities.

Everyone stopped talking when she entered the lobby and stood in its center, looking around with her beaming social smile.

'Who'd like to play bridge?' she asked.

Johnstone was game. Mary Jane thought it a splendid idea and naturally Hubby agreed, so Ma led them into the dining room, where they settled in the booth nearest the kitchen.

'Any poker players here?' asked O'Keefe. He looked at me, but Buff answered yes. Kitty asked what kind of stakes there'd be.

'It'll have to be for matches,' I said. 'You put money on the table and Ma'll throw a fit.'

'So?' said O'Keefe. 'You scared she'll call in the law?'

Buff said matches'd be fine and we could pay off in cash on the sly. So we settled on a nickel per match and moved into the dining room's east side booth, beyond Ma's listening range.

Kitty won the cut for deal and O'Keefe took three of the first four pots. I got the other with a pair of tens. Things were even for a while, but gradually O'Keefe starting building up enough matches to make a kindling pile. He managed to keep from grinning but couldn't help letting us know what a game of skill poker was and how dumb our bets were.

When we began cooling off, Buff started whittling away his pile, pushing hard, talking steady and gloating mean. O'Keefe got more and more sullen and several times told Buff to shut up and play. Buff apologized and, what was worse, began sympathizing.

Kitty, I noticed after a while, was winning steadily. She never seemed to take the big pots, never crowed over her success or bitched about the draw. All she did was play her cards and keep saying, 'Raise five.'

Buff was dealing when O'Keefe got three straight deuces up in five card stud. Slowly he counted the matches in his pile. He still had forty-five. He looked at Kitty's hand. She had two kings and a five showing.

'How about we forget about these stupid matches?' said O'Keefe.

'Why not?'

'Ten bucks?'

She glanced at me. I folded. Buff did likewise.

Kitty said she'd see it out.

Buff dealt the last cards. O'Keefe got an ace, Kitty a deuce. She smiled for the first time all evening.

'I'm supposed to figure you've got a king in the hole, right?' said O'Keefe.

'It's not a deuce,' she promised.

'Twenty says it's not a king.'

'I'll take that,' she said, slipped the deuce under the down card's corner and flipped

146

over the king of spades.

O'Keefe said, 'Shit, I should've stayed in jail.'

He stood up, dug out his wallet and tossed two twenties on the table.

'That covers me,' he said and left.

I looked at Buff, who was thoughtfully counting his match pile. Kitty folded the bills and tucked them down the front of her dress.

'I guess you two have played together before,' I said.

'A time or two,' said Kitty.

I strolled back to the west booth and found Ma and Johnstone playing partners and obviously, from their expressions, winning. Mary Jane looked cheerful, but Hubby was suffering. None of them paid me any mind and as I started back toward the lobby Kitty took my arm. When we were in the dimly lighted hall she leaned close and said, 'Come see me later, okay?'

'You're gonna make me a winner?'

'You bet.'

I said I'd be around and watched as she climbed the stairs.

Buff was sitting in the lobby beside the newspaper table, thoughtfully studying the colorful floor. Boswell sat across from him, serenely smoking, hands folded over his ash-strewn lap.

'O'Keefe's really sore,' I told Buff.

'I know.' He wasn't concerned.

'What're you going to do when you get out of the navy?'

He shrugged.

'You're not a career man, huh?'

'Shit, man, the navy's not a career, it's a sentence.'

'You stay AWOL much longer, you'll find out what a real sentence is.'

'Okay, I'm turning myself in. To you.'

I thought that over and decided it was probably the best way to go but didn't know what to do about it for the moment.

'You gonna put me in jail?' he asked.

'Just consider yourself confined to quarters.'

'Okay. I wasn't going anywhere anyway.'

I sat down beside Boswell and stared at Buff, who was looking self-satisfied.

'Why'd you hate Foote?' I asked.

That jolted him and he took a couple seconds before answering.

'What makes you think I hated him?'

'It's plain as hell. But not why.'

He tilted the rocker back and scowled.

'Okay. I just got sick of him being such a lousy phony. All the time pretending he was really our pa, trying to cash in on it—'

'How's that?'

'Well, for Christ's sake, when Ma died he actually told Kitty and me we'd be closer because all we had now was each other. That was worse than nothing—'

'What'd Kitty think?'

'Oh, shit,' he said, getting up. 'She figured we owed him.'

He walked to the window, came back, sat next to me and turned the rocker so we were close.

'She always told me he was good to Ma, but why not? She was beautiful—he was ugly. She cooked, cleaned and washed and took care of us all. She could've done a million times better than sticking with that little creep.'

'From what I hear, she didn't always stay home. She made trips now and then, didn't she?'

'So what? She needed to get away once in a while. What the hell's wrong with that?'

'Who took care of you and Kitty when she was gone?'

He slumped back, scowling.

'There was always somebody—girls or old women. Girls during the days mostly. One old woman even slept over. She might've slept with old Foote for all I know.'

'How long'd your ma be gone?'

He twitched irritably. 'I don't remember. Usually it seemed like forever, but you know how kids are. They think any time is forever when they're waiting. Like it seems to me I was in grade school for a million years.'

I rolled a smoke and lit up while he sat there brooding. It made him self-conscious,

149

knowing I was watching. He pulled in his lower lip to give his mouth a firm line.

'I know Foote got a check every month,' I said. 'Did Kitty get money too?'

He stared at me in open surprise.

'What would she get money for?'

'I don't know what Foote got it for—do you?'

For half a second I thought he was going to say yes, then he got a cautious look and shook his head.

'Haven't you thought about it?'

'Not really.' He was very casual. He stared at the floor a moment or two and then slid his glance my way. 'You got a notion?'

'Yeah. I think somebody was sweet on your ma but had a wife and couldn't ditch her. When your ma got pregnant this guy got her to marry Foote and the payments were to take care of the kid and let them move out of Aberdeen. And every so often this sugar daddy wanted her again and he'd give her a vacation.'

I thought he'd get mad but he only turned more thoughtful.

'Yeah, it could have been like that. I think I was the result of one of those vacations. A vacation baby. That's a nice notion, huh?'

He suddenly became aware of Boswell puffing on my other side and leaned forward to look at him.

'How about it, Professor, who do you think

the sugar daddy was?'

'Prob'ly a traveling man,' said Boswell.

Buff grinned, then laughed.

'It figures, it really figures. I do like that. A traveling man.'

'Did Azalea go on a trip before the last baby was born?' I asked.

He stopped laughing.

After a little thought he shook his head. 'I don't know. I was just a little kid then. Ask Kitty, she might know.'

'Do you remember if Foote shared a bed with your ma?'

He didn't want to think about that. He said ask Kitty.

'It could've been him, you know. Women let men in for all kinds of reasons—it doesn't have to be all romance. Just being around at the right time's all it takes about three times out of four.'

'Jesus,' he said in disgust, 'you *are* old, aren't you?'

'I've been around awhile,' I admitted. 'It could be she got fond of old Foote. That might be the reason the poor bastard died so hard. Whoever did it either thought they had to learn something from him, or it was a hate killing.'

He stared at me for a long moment.

'You actually think maybe I did it, don't you?'

'Did you?'

He settled back, tilted the rocker, folded his arms and shook his head.

'If it'd been me, I wouldn't have left him hanging there for just anybody to find. I'd have dragged him to a railroad ditch or someplace like that and covered him with snow so he wouldn't be found till spring, when I was off someplace. I sure's hell wouldn't have stuck around for the goddamned funeral.'

'Did you think about it when you were a kid?'

'No. I enjoyed thinking about him being dead. I really liked that idea. But little kids don't think about killing grown-ups. I mean, hell, it's like thinking about killing God. You just don't know how to manage it, you know?'

I'd thought about it. I thought of a wire across the first step on the cellar for Elihu or of using the gun he kept in the lobby desk. I even hefted the gun and found it weighed a ton. I thought of waiting on the balcony for him to pass under and dropping something heavy at the right moment. Only anything I thought would do the job was too heavy to carry unnoticed up the stairs.

So I nailed his slippers to the floor and left a tack on his swivel chair and stapled his cap to the wall peg. All that got me was whalings, and my only satisfaction was in knowing I'd tried to get back at him for not liking me.

'Ever get to Pearl Harbor?' I asked Buff.

'Yeah, we got in there a couple of times.'

'I was on the beach there for a while.'

'No shit? When?'

'About six years ago.'

'I've heard of guys doing that—how was it?'

'After three years in the army, it was damned fine for the first six months.'

'You get lots of wahines?'

'A few.'

For several seconds he got all excited and asked questions, but pretty soon it seemed to depress him.

'I'd be afraid,' he admitted. 'Most of those girls, they've got the clap, haven't they?'

'I never took a poll, but none of them ever gave it to me.'

He shook his head. 'If I'd tried, I'd have got a dose sure.'

I noticed Boswell was dozing off and suggested he go upstairs and sack out. It took a while but eventually he managed and headed up the steps with hardly a stagger. The bottle on his hip would insure good sleep and I thought of the fine restraint he'd shown since coming to the hotel.

'How old is he?' Buff asked when I sat down again.

'I never asked.'

'He must be damned old.'

'That's no great crime.'

153

He didn't grant that.

'Did Foote ever make a pass at Kitty?' I asked.

He'd been leaning forward in the rocker, staring at the floor. The question jerked him up, glaring.

'He wouldn't have dared!'

I met his eyes until he looked away and settled back. Upstairs somebody coughed and a chair scraped the floor. My mind wandered to Kitty alone in her bed in fourteen. Maybe wondering why I hadn't shown up. No, not likely. It was too early yet.

'Kitty ever go for young, good-looking guys?' I asked.

He thought that over, sighed and said he guessed so. She had pretty much gone for Greg Plant awhile there. And there had been some others, none of them amounted to much.

'Nobody's ever been good enough for her as far as you're concerned, right?'

'That's right.'

He looked up at the clock. It was just about to haul off and strike ten. We watched until the minute hand hit twelve and the strokes began. It had a fine, positive sound. Nothing equals a clock for positive, no matter how far it's off.

We were still listening to the silence that followed when O'Keefe came down the stairs, stopped by the hall for his coat and came out

154

on his way to the door.

'Going to the pool hall?' I asked.

He halted, still buttoning his coat and tilted his head at me.

'You figure on stopping me?'

'I don't have much choice. The judge wants you whole when you come around in the morning.'

'You're not holding any pool cue now,' he told me, 'and there's no crowd backing you up.'

'That's right. But I still got all this law on my side. You better think about that.'

He grinned. 'You want to come outside and weigh that law a little?'

'Wouldn't mind a bit, but do you think that's going to go over big with the judge in the morning?'

He shook his head in mock sadness.

'And here I figured you was a fighter, not a talker.'

'And I thought you had a little sense. You tired of working for Johnstone?'

He started unbuttoning his coat.

'You're a slick article, Wilcox. One of these days you and me'll have a go at it.'

'Seems likely.'

He grinned even more and started toward the hall as Johnstone and Ma came in from the dining room. Ma had the glow of a winner and Johnstone's hand was on her elbow until he saw us.

He looked at O'Keefe and scowled. 'Going somewhere?'

'Gonna hang up my coat,' said O'Keefe.

Johnstone looked at me with his eyebrows raised. Ma excused herself, saying she had to go check on Elihu. The thought made her feel guilty, and her glow melted away as she bustled toward the bedroom.

Johnstone walked to the window and said over his shoulder. 'The snow's letting up. Plows ought to be through by morning.'

He turned to face me.

'If they do their job, we'll leave after breakfast.'

'First O'Keefe sees the judge.'

'Of course. But then we leave.'

'That'll be up to the judge.'

CHAPTER FOURTEEN

It was eleven-thirty before I crawled in with Kitty. We didn't talk any until after, but then she propped herself on one elbow and leaned close.

'If Johnstone goes back to the Cities tomorrow, I'll be going along.'

She waited for me to say something and finally I told her I'd miss her.

'Sure,' she laughed softly. 'But you really won't give a damn, will you?'

156

'I never figured you'd stay.'

She lowered her head until I could feel her warm breath.

'I'm still going to break up with him. I've had enough of all that. He's been good to me, but it's just gone on too long for where it can go.'

'You trying to convince me or you?'

She pulled back a little. 'God knows I sure didn't expect any help from you. You're lots of fun, but somehow you're never all there—you know what I'm saying?'

'I put all I've got there.'

She pinched my nose hard.

'That's not what I'm talking about and you know it. I'm just a roll in the hay for you, like any other bimbo.'

'No. You're something special. But you never planned on anything permanent with me.'

She laid her head on my chest and sighed.

'It *has* been fun. I'd heard so much and really was curious.'

She lifted her head and kissed me on the mouth. I took hold of her and kissed back and she squirmed around until she was on top full length.

'You too sleepy?' she asked.

'I thought I was...'

She squirmed some more. 'I don't think so.'

It turned out she was right and sometime

later when she had settled down with her nose between the hollow of my neck and shoulder, I asked if it was lonely at the top. She said not that she could remember.

I drifted off for a few seconds.

'Carl?' she said.

'Uh-huh?'

'You want to talk?'

'Uh-huh.'

'I do. Okay?'

'Sure.'

'I'm scared about all this.'

I opened my eyes and looked into the darkness.

'All what?'

'The murders. Thinking back. Not knowing so many things. I think about Mom and what life was like for her, living in our crummy little house and thinking about the trips she took and what things might've been like for her if she hadn't got pregnant with me. You should've seen her. She was really pretty. Not movie-star, phony pretty, but, I don't know—I thought she was truly beautiful. Her hair was all golden and shiny and long. Most of the time she had it all up in a bun, but before she'd take a trip she'd wash it and brush it and it was gorgeous. Her eyes always seemed to get bigger and bluer with anticipation and her skin would glow—'

'And you'd know she was going to be gone soon?'

'Yeah. It always scared me. I thought she might never come back. I told her that once. She hugged me and said I was silly, how could she not come back to her Kitty, Buff and funny old Arthur?'

'How'd she really feel about him? Arthur, I mean.'

'Oh, she treated him like a big old dog. Only instead of scratching him between his ears or patting his back she'd muss his hair or massage his shoulders.'

'Buff makes it sound like they could hardly stand each other.'

'Poor Buff. He never could stand Arthur. But, of course, the fact is, later on, when he was big enough to understand, things did start going to hell. Something happened when Mom had Baby. I think it all started as soon as she got pregnant with her.'

'Like what?'

'Like everything. They ran out of conversation. Buff was always sullen, Mom got snappish and Arthur just kind of retreated. He'd just leave the house.'

'You got any idea who the man was who used to send for your mother?'

'Yeah,' she said after a moment. 'I've got an idea. But it's pretty crazy.'

'Tell me about it.'

'No, it's too crazy.'

I tried to work on her but she was too tired, or said she was, and after a while she was

159

asleep. I got up, dressed and left.

CHAPTER FIFTEEN

A little after 9.00 A.M. I was sitting in Elihu's swivel chair before the east window when a horse and sleigh pulled up out front, carrying three men. Christenson was driving. He owned a farm west of Corden, still had his heavy Norwegian accent, went to the Lutheran church every Easter and Christmas and somehow, despite drought and grasshoppers, managed to feed his family and make a little money too. His horse, like its master, was big, lean and tough. The passengers climbed down, one tall and spare, the other short and stocky. The short one sank to his knees in the fresh snow but waved off his anxious partner and glanced at the hotel with bright, dark eyes. Once the tall man had pulled their suitcases from the sled, he reached up to shake hands with Christenson and spoke several words. The old Norksy nodded with stoic respect, straightened up, slapped the reins on the horse's back and pulled away.

There was a great bustle as the two men clumped in and Daisy showed up with a broom to whisk snow off their boots and pant legs.

160

The short man removed his hat with a flourish and suddenly I knew this had to be Gaylord Plant, the evangelist father of Gregory. Talk heard over the years had made me expect a giant with white hair, a long thin nose and a prophet's glare. The real man was shorter than me, bald as a watermelon and oak stump stocky. His snub nose perched over a wide mouth, his dark eyes were deep set under bushy brows that looked too dark for a man of his years and his gaze took me in with the kind of attention my nephew gives to a piece of cake before he takes his first bite.

'Carl Wilcox,' announced the man. His voice was soft and furry as a rabbit.

I confessed to the name.

'How's Elihu?'

'Compared to what?'

His smile was indulgent.

'I'm told he's had a stoke.'

'He survived.'

The reverend's glowing eyes bored into me while he tried to decide whether I was being insubordinate toward him or my old man. Either way, he wasn't pleased.

'I remember him as a strong man,' he said.

'He was.'

The reverend removed his heavy coat, handed it to his man and stood with his stocky legs spread, like Ahab on the bridge.

'I'm Gaylord Plant, and this,' he jerked his head toward the coat bearer, 'is my assistant,

Clint Cogswell. I want room two.'

I said okay and walked behind the register as they approached.

Plant picked up the pen, glanced at the last name entered and froze just a second before quickly stroking his signature above that of his dead son's. He added a Minneapolis address and handed the pen to Cogswell before nailing me once more with his warm, dark eyes.

'I don't expect you remember me,' he said. 'When I was here last you were about eight years old. Had a bandage over your nose, which had been broken by a boy who hit you with a slingshot.'

'It was a rock, actually. Of course, it started from a slingshot.'

'Why'd he do it?'

'He took me for Goliath.'

'On a barn roof?'

'Kids have lots of imagination.'

He decided I was an innocent kidder and suddenly offered me a forgiving smile.

'I gather, from what I've heard, that you've had a rather adventurous life ever since.'

'You gather that from Christenson?'

'Mr. Christenson,' he said, 'is a most phlegmatic man. Not given to gossip. His wife, on the other hand, is a fount of information.'

'Which you scooped up?'

'Hungrily,' he said, letting me know he

wasn't above a little kidding himself.

He looked around the lobby, taking in the leather-upholstered rockers, the big table under the clock with its pile of newspapers and the floor covered with linoleum, which Elihu had recently painted yellow and stippled with red and brown. The reverend blinked.

'The old man figured yellow'd brighten the place up,' I said.

'It does that.'

He wandered over to the green canary cage, where yellow Dick perched. The bird gave a self-conscious peep and turned his back.

'He's a singer, I'd guess,' said Plant. 'Your father's had canaries all his life, hasn't he?'

'Had two for a while. Then one night some character stole the other one, cage, stand and all.'

'Interesting. I can feel more forgiving of a man who'd steal a songbird than one who'd take a chicken. Does that sound logical?'

'Not very.'

'I suppose not. I'm not basically a logical man. Would it be convenient for me to visit with your father while you and Clint take our bags up to the room?'

I said I'd check with Ma and went into the bedroom while the two new guests hung their coats in the hall.

Ma, of course, went into a tizzy fit when she heard who was with us and started

163

dashing around, straightening up the room, which, except for Elihu, was already neat as a needle. She grabbed a brush and smoothed his wild hair. As soon as she turned away he brought both ancient hands up to see what had happened and restored the fright wig look with two passes.

Ma darted out to greet the great man and I led his partner up the creaking stairs and down the groaning hall.

Cogswell's craggy face showed some relief when he took in the large, L-shaped room with its beds at each end so you couldn't see one from the other. The wallpaper was mostly white and reflected light from outside clear to the deepest corners.

He set his suitcase on the bench at the foot of the bed away from the windows and considered the circular woven rag rug under his feet.

'It's just as the reverend described it,' he said and tilted his head to look down on me. 'He has a remarkable memory, you know.'

I nodded as I set the reverend's suitcase on the stand by the window overlooking First Street.

Cogswell dug a purse from his pocket and poked around in it. I told him where the shower and can were and he said thanks, he'd noticed as we passed them and besides the reverend had told him what to expect.

'Wait,' he said as I edged toward the door.

I waited.

He came within a yard of me, still holding the purse.

'How'd it happen? I mean, Gregory's death?'

'Somebody coldcocked him, tied him up and dumped him off the fire escape into the snow in back of the hotel.'

'Good Lord! Who?'

'I don't know yet. How'd you and the reverend get to Christenson's?'

'We flew,' he said proudly. He made it sound as if they'd come on angel wings.

'How?'

'Hired a pilot I know. Fellow named Sheppard; you may have heard of him. He's a stunt flier. He has an airplane with skis and we flew from Minneapolis and landed in a pasture, west of town. It was horribly noisy. Have you ever flown?'

'Not yet.'

'It's an exhilarating experience, but awfully cold this time of year. The farmer, Christenson, was amazing. Stolid. Unbelievable. He showed no surprise at our miraculous arrival. His first question was "Would you like a cup of coffee?" And Reverend Plant's response was beautiful. He said we would be delighted. Mrs. Christenson gave us fresh-cooked doughnuts. I wanted to get a room with them, but Reverend Plant wisely decided we should get here as quickly as possible. Which brings me to why I asked you to wait—where's Gregory's body?'

'At the funeral home two blocks east.'

'Is he viewable?'

'I guess so.'

'We'll be taking him to Aberdeen. That's where he was most at home, you know. Being the son of a missionary can be a very difficult life—it was quite out of the question to take the boy along to missions where the reverend served.'

I wished my old man had been a missionary.

'Who's investigating the murder?'

'I am.'

He stared at me for a moment, then smiled. I thought his face would crack, but it didn't quite. 'You're joking.'

'The regular man's sick. I was appointed a couple days ago.'

'But,' he waved, taking in the room and suitcases, 'you're working here—'

'Elihu just had a stroke. I'm filling in the gaps all around.'

'That's incredible ... I understand—'

'Yeah, I'm an ex-con. I served my time, so they don't mind now if I change sides.'

He was still trying to digest that when I asked if he'd heard anything about our earlier murder. He said, yes, Christenson's wife was quite excited about it. Her husband, on the other hand, was remarkably uninterested.

166

'You know where Foote came from?' I asked.

He said no, snapped his purse shut and stuck it in his pocket without meeting my eyes.

'He came from Aberdeen. Same as the reverend and his son. Quite a coincidence, huh?'

He allowed it was a small world.

I asked him how long he'd been with the preacher.

'From the beginning,' he said with swelling pride.

'Of creation?'

'Of my re-creation. I heard his message first in San Francisco. I was part of a small gathering of indifferent people who came out of curiosity and were transformed into a dedicated band of saved souls. That night changed my life forever. With others I went up to him after the sermon, fell on my knees and told him he was my leader. And you know? He was embarrassed. He begged me to rise and did the same to others who followed my example. He had no idea at that moment what he'd accomplished. The others, seeing his embarrassment, drifted off, but I stayed with him, and his wife joined us and we went to a cafe where we drank coffee and talked until the place closed and then we went to his hotel and that's where our crusade began—'

'Yeah. You do any crusading in Aberdeen?'

It took him a second to get back to earth but he tried to put a good face on it and allowed that yes, they'd been to Aberdeen a couple times.

'Ever meet a woman named Azalea?'

That turned him thoughtful. He repeated the name after a moment and said, very casually, he wasn't sure—what was her last name?

'Her married name was Foote. Wife of Arthur, the man who ended up with the barbed wire necktie.'

His high brow furrowed a bit as he gave it deep thought while studying the woven rug at his feet.

'Clint rarely remembers women,' said the reverend as he came in behind me. His voice had lost some of its furriness; it almost had an edge.

He walked a short circle, looking the room over and finally sat down on the bed near the window and pierced me with his brown eyes.

'You should be making peace with your father,' he told me.

'He tell you we were at war?'

'You are alienated. He doesn't have much time, you know. He needs your acceptance and, God knows, you need his. Is it true that you've stopped drinking?'

'I haven't taken any pledge, no.'

He sighed. 'You wouldn't. You're a stiff-necked pair.'

I grinned at him.

'What's the matter, Reverend? Wasn't he ready to be saved?'

That didn't amuse him a lot, but he managed a gentle smile that showed white teeth. For some reason he made me think of God and I tried to remember any picture I'd ever seen that showed either God or Christ smiling. I couldn't remember any. I suppose when you're almighty you know too much to smile.

'I told him,' he said, 'I was going to ask you to come down and visit with him. I told him he owed it to himself and to you to reach an understanding, an acceptance of each other.'

'He agree?'

He shook his bald head soberly.

'He told me I'd have more luck mating a dog and a cat.'

'So he's not as far gone as you thought. Tell me, what do you remember about Azalea?'

He frowned, crossed his short legs and held the upper one in place with both hands resting on his ankle.

'She came up to the altar when I called the sinners forward during our first crusade in Aberdeen after Clint joined me. Her maiden name was Larson. She was remarkably pretty despite her dowdy clothes. I learned she'd been orphaned as a little girl and grew up as the ward of a well-to-do family that treated her like an indentured servant. I suspect she took some handling. She was a highly spirited girl, very fair and small. Later on she married Arthur Foote. Back then he owned a jewelry store and watch-repair shop in downtown Aberdeen.'

I asked if Foote had been with Azalea when she came up to the altar and he said, no, she'd been alone.

'Did you meet Foote back then?'

He had. He'd decided to buy a watch and went into Foote's shop near the hotel. He intended to pick something cheap and reliable but while looking around sighted a handsome Longines and couldn't resist asking its price and handling it. In response to his questions, Foote agreed that the watch would be accurate, durable and a reflection of his own responsibility and worth. Of course, he said, he would be happy to give the preacher a discount.

I said it sounded as if Foote had been a good salesman. He should have been doing all right.

Plant laughed. 'The sales job, in this case, was performed by the customer. I wanted that watch and even Foote, who was not truly quick, could see it from the beginning. If he had been shrewd at all, he would never have agreed to a discount.'

Plant had been so pleased with the watch he had made a ritual of returning to the shop each time he returned to Aberdeen.

'When did he close the place?' I asked.

He wasn't sure or even particularly interested. He said he went back one year and found it was out of business.

'You don't remember what year?'

He said no impatiently.

'You know when he married Azalea?'

'I never heard. Are you going down to talk with your father?'

'In a minute. I thought you kept track of everything. How come you can remember every detail of a room like this but don't know what happened to people you were interested in?'

'Rooms don't change or move. People do. I think Foote went out of business because he preferred puttering to handling the responsibilities it entailed. He liked to repair watches. You don't get far in this world if you don't promote new business—that's a lesson you should learn.'

'I guess you've got it down pat.'

He let his ankle free, lowered his foot to the floor and placed his hands on his knees.

'To be honest, no. That's handled by Clint. He's my business manager, the practical man. He prepares my schedules, arranges for the halls I talk in, the tents we need, the interviews. Back in our headquarters, in Minneapolis, they say, if Gaylord Plant died, no one would notice, but if anything happened to Clint Cogswell, the entire crusade would end. The fact is, I was never anything until Clint came into my life. I didn't even understand what a message I had. Passionate preachers are all over this land, but competent managers are rare as frog hair. Go talk with your father, Carl.'

I walked to the door and stopped to look back.

'Did it surprise you when Foote married Azalea?'

His eyes narrowed as he tilted his bald head.

'Not much, no. Of course, I heard about it quite a while after the last time I saw either of them. She never had a father, you know, maybe she needed one. Arthur was a gentle man. She needed someone to bring serenity into her life. I suspect it was a blessed union. Certainly it was fruitful.'

'Neither of their kids think he fathered them.'

He stared at me for a moment, got up, went around to his suitcase and began unstrapping the clamps.

'Children are often imaginative about their parents,' he said over his shoulder. 'They make things up.'

Clint moved over beside the reverend as the old man opened the case and said, 'Let me.'

For a second I caught a glimpse of exasperation as the preacher turned his face, then it was gone. He backed off a step, still facing the suitcase.

'How many kids did you have?' I asked.

He turned his thick body from the hips and shot me cold with his eyes.

'One,' he said and turned to the window. 'The one I came here to bury.'

'How'd you hear of the death?'

'Someone called—'

'Who?'

He turned to Clint.

'A woman,' he said. 'Kitty Foote.'

I nodded and then asked the reverend if he'd ever met Foote's daughter or son. He hunched his shoulders and said no.

'They both have hair like their mother's, but their eyes are brown. Foote had blue eyes.'

The preacher turned slowly and looked at Clint.

Clint excused himself and went out, closing the door.

The preacher folded his short arms and leaned his shoulder against the windowsill.

'All right. You've got a notion. Tell me about it.'

I dug out my fixings and started rolling a smoke.

'It's more like a wild hair than a notion.'

He kept watching me.

'Did you know your son made love to Kitty?' I asked.

173

His mouth sagged, like a man taking a hook to the gut, then he clinched his jaw and glared.

'Where? When?'

'Five, maybe six years ago. At your brother's place in Minneapolis.'

He pushed his jaw at me.

'How'd you know about this?'

'She told me.'

'My dear God.' He lowered his head and slowly rubbed his bald dome with one hand. Suddenly he looked up. 'Did she—?'

'No. She was lucky. No kid.'

'She told you this too?'

'Uh-huh.'

'Well, it seems you have quite a talent for obtaining confidences.'

I shrugged modestly.

'And for surprises. Your timing's good. Very deliberate.'

I lit my cigarette and he watched the smoke rise slowly in the still room. Outside the wind moaned. He turned to stare through the window and clasped his thick, liver-spotted hands behind his back. The palms were pink and pillow soft.

'This is a melancholic country,' he said. 'When I left it, I never intended to return. Never.'

'Yeah, but we all seem to.'

'Yes.' He nodded his head. 'Penance, I suppose. And family. Gregory was stubbornly

174

attached to the town where he was born.'

He turned and without looking my way, moved over to the bed and sat down.

'I never really wanted to leave him behind back in the old days when I went out on my missions. But it was out of the question. He was so small and it was pitilessly primitive where we went. I watched children die by the hundreds in Africa. No medicines, sanitation ... I'd have taken him along later, when we toured in the states, but his mother persuaded me it'd be bad for him—that he should stay in one school, keep his friends, live a normal life. You know, I dreamed of seeing him in my audience, watching me with the eyes of love that my people offer everywhere—but it was never like that. The few times he *was* out there, he avoided my eyes. I embarrassed him. That's a humbling experience, I can tell you.'

He sighed deeply, shook his gleaming head and gave me a sad smile.

'Talk with your father, Carl. Don't miss your chance.'

'How about your wife? She ever want to stay home and lead a normal life?'

'She was a Rachel. Where I went, she went. My mission was hers.'

'Was she Irish?'

'Swedish. One hundred percent.'

'Like the Vikings?'

'Their women went on no raids.'

'No, they just wore the stolen jewelry.'

'You're deliberately badgering me, aren't you? What is it you're after? I'm a betrayed father—you should show some respect for that if nothing else.'

'You don't seem that interested in your son. You've shown more interest in what gives between Elihu and me than in what happened to your own kid.'

He smiled. Forgiveness spread all over his map. The calculation in it galled me.

'You haven't even asked what happened,' I said, 'and don't tell me you got all the facts from Mrs. Christenson—the grapevine's good around here but not that good. You want to know what really happened?'

His eyes turned cold.

'Tell Clint. He'll be making the arrangements. He takes care of everything.'

I stared at him and he glared back.

'You want me to probe the sordid details? To cry out for justice, retribution, revenge? I won't. He's dead. I accept that as God's will. Whatever Gregory did to bring this on himself was beyond me. God knows and He understands and I leave it to Him. Don't try to trick or trap me or imply that somehow I'm responsible for this tragedy. If I am, that's between my God and me. It's not your concern. Look to your own responsibilities, man, you've never faced them, you're in no position to take the lofty plain—'

'Did Clint arrange the trust for Foote?'

His head jerked, then he clamped his jaw firm and stared at me.

'You know what I'm talking about,' I said. 'The little settlement to help Azalea out and give Arthur a way to support her and the bastard kid in a new town.'

He took a deep breath, stood up, walked to the window and after a moment turned to face me.

'It was a piece of impulsive philanthropy. Nothing more. She came to me for help. I've done similar things for others. There was nothing base or disgraceful about it and it has no relationship with what's happened here this week. Now, I ask you one more time, go and talk with your father. And on the way, tell Clint I would like to see him. You and I will talk later, but now, please send Clint to me.'

It was the first time he'd said please in my hearing and it impressed me. More questions came to mind, but I figured he wouldn't answer, so I said, okay, he could depend on it, we'd talk later.

Clint was in the lobby, pretending to read a week-old newspaper while listening to Jack brag to Mary Jane.

He looked up at me and lowered the paper when I stopped in front of him. His pale eyes took me in serenely.

'He wants you,' I said.

177

He nodded, folded the paper once, set it carefully on the stack under the clock and started toward the stairs.

'Was the trust your idea?' I asked as he passed under the arch.

He halted with his hand on the bannister.

'Trust? I don't understand. We've always had trust. That isn't an idea, that's a relationship.'

I smiled.

'Maybe you had it once. Now maybe you've got something else. Go see the man, he's waiting.'

He went up without looking back. I couldn't be sure whether he climbed slower or quicker than usual but had a feeling he wished he had more flights to climb.

CHAPTER SIXTEEN

Ma was in the bedroom sitting on the short-backed, seat-sprung dressing table chair that suited her Puritan soul. She started at the sight of me because I caught her gazing out the window at the drifted snow under the rows of clothesline. To let me know she hadn't been lollygagging she snatched up her needlework and remarked, 'Well! He said you'd come.'

'That doesn't make him a prophet.'

She frowned and glanced at Elihu just as he opened his eyes to take in the ceiling for a confused moment. Then he rolled his head slowly and piped me.

I expected him to ask if I'd shoveled the walk yet, but he only stared as if I were a stranger, then tried to clear his throat and coughed a couple times. Finally he asked how Daisy was doing.

'Okay. So's Bertha.'

He blinked thoughtfully and asked how many guests we had now?

'Lost one, gained two.'

'Good. Just keep that up regular and we'll pay the bills.'

Ma stood, set her work on the seat she'd abandoned and walked over to stare down at him.

'He needs a shave. You can do it.'

I didn't like the notion. It kind of suited me to see him looking scruffy for a change, but the worst thing was I remembered what happened when barbers worked on him. For years whenever he could find one who'd never seen him before, he'd get up in the chair and bet the barber he couldn't shave him without drawing blood. And every time the boobs would take the bet, warm Elihu's tough whiskers with hot towels, strop their razors till they hummed and lay on soap with a hot brush. After the first pass they'd start to grin, but even as they started on the second stroke they'd spot blood beginning to seep, ever so gently, through the parchment skin while the old man grinned.

'Right now,' I told Ma, 'I don't think he can spare the blood.'

'It won't be that bad if you're careful. It's got to be done.'

'Better dead than ugly, huh?'

'He can't keep his spirits up when he looks like a tramp.'

I didn't bother to tell her he had no notion how he looked. It was her spirits that needed keeping up.

'Okay. I'll shave him.'

She said good and went out to help Bertha start lunch.

Elihu's eyes opened as I sat down on the edge of the bed.

'You know me?' I asked.

He scowled. 'Of course.'

'You remember the old claim?'

The watery blue eyes brightened a little.

'Sure. South a ways from here. Good, flat land. No rocks. Clay down deep but good soil on top—'

'And our crops went to grasshoppers, prairie fire and drought. That make sense to you?'

He closed his eyes and opened them again. 'Yeah. Kind of. Don't anything good come easy, you know. That's how it's supposed to be. It would've worked out in the end but

180

your ma wouldn't have been happy. She never minded the work none, or even the wind all that much, but she wanted company and style and a doctor nearby when he was needed...'

The short history tired him and he drifted off.

I went to the kitchen, got a hot kettle of water, came back, filled the bowl by the side table, got out his shaving kit and, after waking him, spread a towel under his head, lathered his face and went to work with the razor. Blood came, but I didn't press and it wasn't bad. He half dozed through it.

It was a weird experience. I couldn't remember the last time I'd touched that face. Maybe I never had.

When I was through and had rinsed him off and patted his jowls down with cool water, he rested quietly with his eyes closed.

'That preacher,' he said at last, 'he thinks I'm gonna go.'

'Preachers always say we're about to go. It's their stock-in-trade.'

'This ain't no ordinary preacher. His boy's been murdered and he's worrying about an old man he don't hardly know at all.'

'Uh-huh. I'll tell you something. This preacher's worried about a whole lot of things.'

He thought about that awhile and then said, 'He's awful bald, isn't he?'

181

'Yeah. Got a great head of skin.'

He grinned a little, then turned thoughtful again.

'I got to take a crap.' The admission embarrassed him but he tried to pretend it didn't.

'You want me to help you upstairs?'

'It'd beat the thunder mug.'

'I'll carry you.'

'No, just gimme your shoulder.'

He started the struggle of sitting up and was impatient when I moved to help but had to accept it and muttered 'Damnation!' several times before we got his legs over the edge of the bed. When he stood his legs caved in and he sagged against me.

'Dammit, man, stand straight,' he commanded.

'The hell with this,' I said and swung my right arm under his knees and picked him off the floor.

'No!' he yelled. 'I'm not a damned baby—'

'You want to squat over the slop jar with me holding you straight—or do you want to let me take you up where you can sit on the toilet like a man while I wait outside?'

He clinched his jaw and tears squeezed out and flowed down his cheeks as he shook his head and said, 'Shit, O dear God, shit!'

I pushed the French doors open, carried him through the parlor, took a quick peek down the hall and hiked up the stairs as fast as I could move. He wasn't heavy enough to slow me a step.

Luckily the bathroom was unoccupied and I was able to take him in, hold him up while he pulled down his pyjama pants and lower him onto the seat.

I went out, closed the door and leaned against the wall.

It was a long wait. I guessed he wouldn't want to call me and have a lot of yelling back and forth, so I waited till I figured he was okay and opened the door a crack.

'You make it?'

'No, dammit. I'll flush the damned thing when I'm ready.'

I said fine and shut the door.

When he was all squared away I took him down the servants' stairs and made it to his room without anybody's seeing us. Once in the bed Elihu gave a long sigh and turned his head toward the wall.

'Lunch'll be soon,' I told him.

'You got time to shovel the walk,' he muttered.

I went out and shoveled the damned walk.

The sky was solid blue, the snow so white it made my head ache from squinting and there wasn't a puff of wind. In about thirty seconds my hands began to ache with the cold and my nose and cheeks were stinging with the chill. The night wind had packed the snow, so I had to cut it into chunks and I could've built a castle with the blocks I piled along the walk and tumbled into the street.

I'd reached the corner by the time Daisy shoved the storm door open and hollered that lunch was on.

Ma had decided it'd be cozier to have us in booths along the south wall instead of around the center table. That way she got to sit with the preacher, his man Clint and Johnstone. The young couple teamed up with Kitty and Buff, which left me with Boswell and O'Keefe, an arrangement that only Boswell didn't resent.

'There's one sharp old son of a bitch,' O'Keefe told me, jerking his head toward the preacher's booth. 'Got the greatest damn racket in the world. Every yahoo in the country's dying to hand him every dime they've got and he just keeps that old hand out there, telling 'em it's for the glory of God.'

'You figure he's doing better than Johnstone?'

'Hell yes, he makes more of everything, including twitchies, you can bet on it.'

'Maybe Johnstone ought to switch rackets. He's better looking than Plant, might do twice as well.'

'He does all right.'

'Yeah, but can he stay out of jail?'

He squinted at me with his mean eyes. 'What the hell're you trying to get at?'

'I suppose he'll stay out of jail as long as he's got you.'

'What the hell're you getting at?'

'If anybody gets caught, it'll be you, the dog robber.'

He glared as I smiled sweetly.

'Come on,' I said. 'He doesn't keep you around because of your beauty and charm. You're the guy that handles the rough stuff. You keep him from getting his hands dirty.'

'I handle pipsqueaks like you. Now and again some hay shaker feeds me a little shit, but in the long run I come out on top. You'll find that out, buster.'

'Yeah, well, I try to learn a little as I go along.'

He shoved his plate away, got out his cigarette pack and lit one while watching me.

'What'd you get nailed for, Wilcox? Stealing baby's bottles?'

'Once it was for cattle rustling.'

'More like chicken stealing.'

'No, I'm not big on chicken. Strictly a beef man.'

He started to make another crack but suddenly the preacher was standing by our booth and we all looked up at him.

'You talk with your father?' he asked me.

'I started to but he had to go to the can so I carried him up to the toilet.'

He stared at me for a moment, then glanced at O'Keefe and Boswell. Boswell smiled. The preacher smiled back and turned to me again.

'I was hoping you'd have some meaningful dialogue.'

'We've never managed that. Now and again we talk a little—'

'I'd imagine he'd resent being carried like a baby.'

'He didn't complain about that.'

'I think you enjoyed his humiliation.'

I got up. It was nice to talk with a man I could look down at. Okay, so it was a fraction of an inch, it still was down.

'You figure it'd been better if I'd set him on the thunder mug in the middle of the bedroom and held him straight while he took a crap? I took him up where I could leave him to do it alone like a man while I waited outside. No, he wasn't nuts about it. He's not nuts about being helpless and having to lay on his back while some sanctimonious ass preaches at him when he can't get away and tells him he's dying and he's gotta make peace with a son he never gave a damn about. You got a problem because you never settled things with your kid—but that's your problem, preacher. You just make peace with your own God and leave us the hell alone.'

He took all that in without blinking and, when I moved off, followed me into the empty lobby. I parked in Elihu's chair and pulled out my cigarette fixings. The preacher

186

settled in the nearest rocker, turned it a little and tipped his head back as he gripped the armrests.

'In a way,' he said softly, 'you're right. I'll confess that I relate the problems between you and your father with mine and Gregory's. My son's death has made me very aware of my failings as a father. I'll even admit that you and your father pose an irresistible challenge. You're both so far from believing in the truths that are everything to me that I *have* to try to reach you. I realize the timing is impossible, that you can't begin to understand me or my message. But I have to try. We all have patterns in our lives that we can't break free of...'

O'Keefe drifted in, followed by Boswell.

The preacher looked up, tried to be cordial and fell short. He turned to me.

'Where can we talk in private?'

'What're we going to talk about?'

'What you want to know.'

'What do you figure that is?'

'Things you believe are related to these murders.'

'We'll go in the parlor.'

CHAPTER SEVENTEEN

I sat on the chair in the parlor's northeast corner where I could see anyone approaching from the lobby. The preacher perched on the corner of the couch to my right, rested his left elbow on the arm and leaned toward me.

'I knew Azalea. Knew her in the biblical sense. And, yes, I fathered Kitty. Gregory never knew that. Neither did Kitty. Their act of incest was committed in total innocence. It was only by God's mercy there was no issue...'

He swallowed, glanced nervously at the door and lifted his head as if it were unbearably heavy.

'I established the trust for Arthur,' he said, without looking at me. 'Azalea insisted on having the baby. She told Arthur the truth and he was quite happy to marry her knowing that. He worshiped her, you know.'

'And he agreed to leave his shop and move off to work for somebody else?'

He nodded, settled back in the couch and faced me. His voice, which had been just above a whisper, gained strength. Some of the dark guilt seemed to lift from him and his mouth relaxed, not in a smile but something close to it.

'Arthur was quite content to let me handle

things. He had never enjoyed the responsibilities of running a business, he needed someone to manage his affairs and he was helplessly in love with Azalea. He was perfectly happy to leave Aberdeen and the shop and have a sure income and live with his dream girl. They were both very happy with my arrangements.'

'You mean Clint's arrangements, don't you?'

He waved his thick hand heavily.

'Under my directions. And I assure you, Clint never knew that any of it was anything but an example of my philanthropic ways—'

'You set up a lot of trusts, huh?'

'No,' he admitted, 'but I did help a good many people—and still do.'

'Okay. You set up the trust, they moved. Then what?'

'Well, that was the end of it—'

'Bullshit, Reverend. You kept in touch, right?'

'Well, yes, that's my nature. I knew Kitty was born all right and that they were getting along.'

'And you had her come and visit you every now and then. Little paid vacations.'

His mouth tightened up again and he stared over my head through the window behind me.

'She told me she had to see me again because she was losing her faith in God. That only I could save her from damnation. And, oh, how I wanted to believe that! I almost convinced myself that we could meet and not sin. That I could restore her faith, shrive our sins and send her back to her little family, saved.'

'Uh-huh. And instead you sent her home pregnant.'

He closed his eyes and bowed his head, no doubt turning to God for strength. It came. He faced me again.

'You don't understand at all. For you, everything's simple. Your relations with women are confined to satisfying your appetite. You know nothing of the soul or fear of eternal damnation—I could almost envy you, but I'd not trade places for immortality!'

'Guilt makes the sin more sweet?'

He shook his head violently.

'Nonsense. It may intensify experience, but it doesn't sweeten anything. Men have a way of placing the highest value on things that demand the highest price.'

'But you couldn't give up on being God's right-hand man for your true love, could you?'

He lifted his chin proudly.

'She wouldn't have it. She believed in me and my mission. It simply was not to be and we both knew it from the beginning, but she wanted to bear my children and when she had, it was over between us. She was stronger than I. That's hard for me to admit, but it's the God's truth. Azalea had her mission, I had mine.'

'And that'd mean losing Clint too, wouldn't it? If you left God, I mean.'

He'd been getting a little glazed up to then, but that question opened his eyes and mouth. In a second they were back to normal and he stared at me as if I'd just shown up to waken him from a dream.

'You despise me,' he said in surprise. 'You really do, don't you?'

I considered telling him he didn't impress me enough for that, but before I could say it he leaned impatiently forward and was off again.

'I'm everything you've rebelled against, am I not? Religion, spirituality—even success. I've all that and feet of clay, so everything I stand for is garbage to you. I stooped, you think, to the sort of lust you thrive on—you spill your seed as casually as you eliminate your waste—the only difference is that the first is fun he said that as if it were the dirtiest word in the language and the second is necessary—'

'I figure they're both necessary, Reverend. Now let's skip all that and you tell me why you've suddenly made your confession.'

He shifted back on the couch, passed his soft hand over his shining head and spoke carefully.

'I want you to understand there was nothing sinister in the trust I established for Arthur. There was absolutely no reason for me, or anyone close to me, to kill that man, let alone my only son. These things had nothing to do with murder. I've seen enough of you, heard enough, to know you're a cunning and persistent man. You'd have found out what I told you eventually—you've already made several shrewd guesses. But you are totally wrong if you suspect Clint or me of any involvement with what's recently happened here.'

'Who gave Azalea the third kid?'

He looked pained.

'I suppose it was Arthur. It would have to be. We never met after Buff was conceived.'

'I hear she went to see you about the time your wife died.'

'No.'

I let him mourn over that a few seconds before asking how he felt about her getting pregnant without him?

He shook his head ruefully and even smiled.

'Betrayed. Even jealous. The ironies . . . I learned of it the week my wife died. Suddenly I was a widower, and it was too late.'

'What if she didn't get pregnant by Foote? What if it was somebody else? Any idea how Foote would've reacted to that?'

'I can't imagine.'

'You think he might've flipped and burned the house down himself?'

'No. Absolutely not. He wasn't a passionate or possessive man. He loved her selflessly, in ways you couldn't understand—'

'Come on, Reverend. They'd lived together all those years, he outlasted you and took your money and knew you'd made him into a permanent pimp. After all that, if she tumbled into the sack with still another guy, he could've gone nuts.'

'Absolutely not. He was an utterly passive man, perfectly safe. I understand people, Carl, they bare their very souls to me. You can't understand a man like Arthur at all. I know how you think and what you're trying to do to me—next you'll be suggesting that Azalea set the fire—'

'Yeah, I've thought about that.'

'It's a ridiculous idea. She had no dark side, no cruelty in her. She was a loving woman. It's possible some man could've taken her by force—but if it happened she'd have kept it to herself and borne the child, delivered and loved it.'

That didn't leave us anything more to say and after a while I thanked him for his time and left him brooding on the couch.

CHAPTER EIGHTEEN

Johnstone and O'Keefe were waiting in the lobby when I came out and after bundling up we headed for the courthouse. Johnstone was looking spiffy as usual and O'Keefe had managed to get his tie straight and his collar buttoned but still looked like a hoodlum.

He muttered at me, wanting to know how come a judge was working Saturday. I told him judges never worked, they just sat in judgment. That didn't crack either one of them up and we walked the three blocks without further chatter. The sun was blinding, our shadows long and the packed snow creaked underfoot.

The judge was in a foul mood. It didn't help any when he heard that Puck refused to make charges and there'd be no damages to pay for at the pool hall.

When I said no, the prisoner had not resisted arrest he said sarcastically that that wasn't too surprising since from what he'd heard I'd jerked up the man's britches so tight it made him a soprano.

That left him with only disorderly conduct against O'Keefe and he tried to make up for it with a fierce lecture against professional bullies and the people who hired them and a few remarks about the good old days when their ilk could be stocked and horsewhipped. Eventually he wound down.

'The fine's twenty-five dollars. Pay the clerk on your way out.'

As he reached for his wallet Johnstone asked if they were free to leave town. The judge told him, with considerable satisfaction, they were not. There was a little matter of murder to be resolved first. Johnstone said that could take a long time.

'Well,' said the judge, 'that will be sorted out. It's still the weekend. Come Monday we'll see how things stand. Good day. And you, Wilcox, I want to talk to you.'

What he wanted was to know what the hell I'd been doing and I lined it all out.

He shook his head.

'I can't keep them here indefinitely, you know. Hell, the sooner they're gone the better I'll like it. Why don't you go over and jaw with Joey some? Between you, maybe you can figure things out. I hear he's feeling a little better.'

He may have been feeling better, but if he'd looked any worse I'd have voted for burial. All I could think of as I sat by his bed was a bloodhound with a hangover. Despite that, he was curious about the case and listened while now and then taking a sip of water from the stand beside the bed and blinking his sad eyes.

I told him about the only people I'd ruled

out as suspects were Elihu, Ma, Daisy and Boswell.

'You left in Bertha?'

'Sure. She's big enough and mean enough.'

'What'd her motive be?'

'Cussedness, mostly.'

He sighed and asked me to go over the whole gang and when I was through he was quiet so long I thought maybe he'd fallen asleep with his eyes open.

'Maybe,' he said at last, 'you'd ought to talk with Rose over at the cafe.'

'Why?'

'Well, a while back she was kind of thick with Buff. Not everybody knows that—'

'I sure didn't—'

'—well, she was. It's kind of complicated. She might be able to tell you some about him.'

I waited until after the noon hour crowd had left and then drifted into the cafe and after a little kidding around corralled Rose in the back booth by the kitchen door and we sat across from each other drinking coffee.

'Joey says you used to be sweet on Buff Foote,' I said.

'It's more like he was sweet on me. He's five years younger, you know.'

'I'd never've guessed it. But why couldn't you be sweet on a younger guy?'

She lifted her cup with both hands, sipped a bit while looking at me over the rim and

196

grinned wryly as she put it down.

'Come on, Carl, you know me. I've got a weakness for older men.'

'You never got weak with me.'

'You never came on strong enough.'

'That's the first time anybody ever accused me of that.'

'Yeah, well, maybe that's why I noticed it so much.'

I gave her some study, trying to figure if she really was coming on to me. Most of my life I've been trying to find those kind of signs and I've learned over time that I see the signs a hell of a lot more often than they're actually posted.

'Rose, old dear, why've I got this notion you're trying to lead me by the nose?'

'Can't imagine.' She gave me a big grin.

'Uh-huh. Did Buff come around to see you when he first got to town?'

'What ever do you mean?'

She looked so innocent I decided Joey'd been wise.

'Did he let you know before he got here that he was coming?'

'Of course not. I never did anything for that kid but serve him pie after a Saturday night dance when he came in here—'

'Horseapples. Joey says there was something between you and he's got no more imagination than a grizzly. He thinks Buff came to your place when he first came to town and so do I. What I want to know is, when?'

She said she didn't know what I was talking about and looked nervously across the room toward the counter where Kip and the boss were sitting.

I built a cigarette, lit it and pushed smoke, all the time watching her. She squirmed, drank coffee and avoided my eyes except for a couple defiant glances.

'You got a problem Rose. You're not just shooting the breeze with your old buddy. I wish that's how it was, but it's not. I'm a cop. That's plain unnatural, but it's a fact right now. And old Arthur was murdered. Somebody beat that poor bastard all to hell and then hung him up with barbed wire like he was a slaughtered hog. I got to find out who did that. If I don't somebody else'll be called in who can do the job and he's gonna go through all the dirty laundry in Corden till he gets to the bottom of things and he won't give a fart who gets hurt along the way. Everybody in Corden'll be a stranger to him. And you know where you could wind up? An accessory to murder. You don't have to have handed over the club or twisted the wire, all you had to do was give aid and comfort to the guy that did it. In fact, all you got to do is keep your mouth shut about facts that might say who did it.'

She'd stopped looking my way the moment I mentioned being a cop and kept fumbling with her cup and taking quick sips until she had nothing left and she was just massaging the cup.

'When did he show up?' I asked.

She shook her head. 'Buff never killed the old man. He'd *never* do a thing like that. He talks crazy sometimes, but it doesn't mean a thing, he's just a hurt kid—'

I told her I thought she was probably right but I had to know everything, so she'd be doing him a favor if she came clean.

She glanced toward the counter again and saw that Kip and her boss had broken up their gabfest and moved off to work. She pushed her hair back, leaned forward, sighed and said, 'Okay. He called me from Sioux Falls—on Wednesday—last week. He said he was coming to town and wanted to see me. I kidded him, you know, saying this was so sudden and stuff like that and he tried to kid back, but it didn't come off. I mean, he sounded funny. Not ha-ha funny, but strange. I asked what was the matter and he said the truth was he was in a little trouble and could I help because there was nobody else in the world he could turn to. I said what about Arthur and he said that was part of the trouble. He'd heard from his sister, Kitty, and she'd told him that their dad hadn't written and nobody knew where he was—'

'Why'd she tell him that? Why wouldn't she call Joey or somebody else in town?'

She shook her head. 'He didn't explain anything and I didn't think to ask. I was more thinking why Buff was suddenly hot for me. I mean, okay, we *did* mess around just after he was out of high school—that was a bad time for me—I'll tell you about that sometime ... Anyway, the two of us had a little thing going there for a couple of months or so. I felt like an idiot because he was *lots* younger, but he was awfully sweet and so *persistent* and seemed so crazy about me. I needed that just then—you remember Barney?'

'Berenson? Yeah—'

'Well, I fell for him and he did me real dirty. Made me think he wanted to marry me and then left me flat. I was so dumb—'

'So what about Buff?'

'Well, he said he wanted to come and stay with me. He knew I had this place of my own and he said he'd been thinking about the two of us living together like we'd always wanted when we used to have to sneak around. He told about dreams he'd had of me and they were so lovely I just finally said, okay, come on.'

'When'd he come?'

'Thursday night. Late. He'd hitched a ride and got to my door, oh, golly, it must've been midnight. A truck driver'd dropped him off just beyond town and he'd walked to my place in only a navy pea jacket and thin gloves. He about froze. When I let him in he looked like a ghost. I got him into a hot tub and warmed soup for him and he was so grateful he just broke down and cried like a baby.'

So she got used again. I reached over and patted her hand, which was flat on the table beside her cup. She didn't pull away and her eyes began to leak slowly. She dug a hanky from her apron pocket with her free hand and wiped her eyes.

I asked if Buff had told her he was AWOL. She nodded.

'You know how long?'

She didn't know that.

'Where'd he been?'

'Lots of places. Minneapolis, for one.'

'Did he ask about Arthur when he first showed up here?'

'Uh, yeah, I think so. Actually he didn't exactly ask *about* him, he just said, sort of casually, he supposed Arthur was still living at Abigail's and I told him he was still missing, like his sister said.'

'How long had he been missing?'

'Oh, since a while after the holidays, I guess. Nobody thought much of it at first because he went on drunks every so often. Abigail always pretended he was off visiting relatives or something because she wouldn't admit he was a drunk. She's death on booze, you know. Usually he went in the summer, when he could sleep it off in a hay field or something.'

'Where'd you learn all this?'

'Where do I learn anything? At the cafe. People talk. I listen.'

'Who talked?'

'Who didn't? Of course, nobody really knew, but they figured things out. Everybody in Corden knew what was going on. You'd know too if you ever stayed around long enough.'

She was right. In Corden word passes like the air and sooner or later everybody knows everything. Of course, half what they know is bullshit, but there are never any complete secrets for long.

Two batches of late lunchers showed up and she left to wait on them. After they gave their orders and she'd passed them on to the kitchen she dropped back to say she'd be busy for a while.

'Okay. How long'd Buff stay with you?'

'Till he went over to the hotel.'

'He been back to see you?'

'He called a coupla times,' she said, glancing toward her customers. 'Didn't say anything. Just trying to be nice.'

'Okay, Rose, you did right, telling me. Don't worry.'

'I won't,' she said, starting to drift away, 'but is it okay if I cry a little?'

CHAPTER NINETEEN

I left the cafe, headed south two blocks to the railway crossing and turned west on the tracks that led over the big hill. The plow had been through, clearing the black rails and, in places where snow had drifted, leaving enormous banks. The low overcast made it seem like I was walking through a gray-roofed tunnel. I was sheltered from the north wind until after about a mile and a half the tracks curved to my right and pretty soon I was taking the brunt of it. By then I was at the crest of the hill and the banks were gone, leaving me exposed as a black ant on a marble counter. I could look a million miles in every direction and see nothing but billowing snow that turned gray in the long distance and blended into the overcast. I spotted the little white schoolhouse, with its clapboard walls and blank windows, sitting about a rod back from the road a quarter of a mile from the tracks. I could also see that the deep ditches flanking the rails were filled with snow and decided it'd be easier to hike an extra half mile along the tracks and double back than to wade through snow up to six feet deep.

The front door, when I finally reached it, was padlocked, but I found a window I could open and crawled inside, closing it behind me.

There was no heat, but getting out of the wind made it seem almost warm and I stood on the bare wooden floor, looking around at the twenty little desks and the one big one, which stood on a little platform at the south end. It was all one big room except for the entryway, which was flanked by cloakrooms, one for boys, the other for girls. The blackboard, which ran along the wall behind the teacher's desk, had been scrubbed clean and erasers and chalk were lined up neatly in the tray below. Across the top was the alphabet in big, clear letters of gold.

There was a white vase on the desk. The potbellied stove stood in the southwest corner and beside it was a big crate filled with split wood.

I tried to imagine where Foote had slept and what the hell he could've done and thought between drinks as he passed days in that bare and silent room. It was beyond me. I couldn't have lasted an hour.

The walk to Christenson's was just over half a mile and I was met at the driveway by his two gray mutts, Tidy and Clean. These were names, not descriptions, and I never could tell them apart. From a good distance a nervous man could mistake them for wolves, but up close they were smaller and scruffier than that and their tails wagged so hard they could hardly keep their rear ends upright. I patted their heads and behinds and they trotted to the house ahead of me as I approached the kitchen stoop.

A blonde young woman opened the inner door and peered out through the storm door glass. Her brows and lashes were light as her hair and there was a skyful of blue in her eyes.

I stopped at the first step of the small back porch and smiled at her. The dogs sat down, flanking me.

She opened the door a crack and said, 'Yes?'

'I'm Carl Wilcox.'

'I know.'

'You're the schoolteacher, Greta, right? I was just over at your schoolhouse. You keep it awful neat.'

'Is that one of your responsibilities now, checking on schoolhouses?'

'No.' I grinned some more. 'I got other problems, but they keep spreading out.'

'Yes.'

'I'd like to talk with you a few minutes.'

She frowned. 'What about?'

'Arthur Foote.'

For a moment I thought she was going to shut the door and leave me standing there with my mouth open. She turned pink, started to speak, lowered her head and said, 'What're you implying?'

'Not a thing. Can I come in and talk?'

'My parents are gone. Father wouldn't approve of me letting a man in the house when I'm alone.'

'So let the dogs in with me. They'll protect you.'

She looked them over with something short of confidence but after another second's hesitation opened the door and stood back as I entered. The dogs stood in place. She didn't call them in.

The kitchen was wide and high with towering cabinets, a cistern pump by the sink, a black wood stove and a rectangular wooden table at dead center surrounded by four straight-backed chairs. The plank floor was scrubbed bone white.

She offered coffee, which I accepted, and stayed on her feet a few minutes before finally sitting down across from me. I made some complimentary remarks about the fine kitchen and the coffee and took great pains not to look her over, which of course I wanted to do. I couldn't remember ever seeing her before and couldn't believe I wouldn't have noticed her looks if I had. She was no beauty, and the paleness of her hair and the blankness that came from eyes that had no decoration seemed unnatural.

I explained why I'd gone over to the school and why I'd come to talk with her.

'The way Foote was murdered, there just has to be something awful complicated involved. I mean, from the little I know about him, he was a sorry old guy who never gave anybody any trouble. He shouldn't have had any enemies, he didn't even have friends. He just wasn't the kind of guy who'd end like he did. And right up until today I didn't know he was a boozer.'

She leaned over her cup. The soft, fair hair fell forward, framing her smooth face. It had a shine that made it look polished. I guessed she brushed her hair a lot.

Without looking up she asked, 'Do you think he suffered very long?'

'You mean when he was killed? Yeah, I'm afraid so.'

She lifted her head slightly. The blue about flooded me.

'You feel sorry for him, don't you?' she said.

'Yeah.'

She nodded and looked into her coffee cup. 'He was the saddest little man I ever met.'

'Tell me about him.'

'It's really nothing. Or wouldn't be for most ... I saw smoke coming out of the school chimney when I got up one morning. I didn't say anything to Dad, but after breakfast I took the dogs and walked over. It was during Christmas vacation, so there was no school. Anyway, I got there and saw the door was padlocked like I'd left it and I went around and peeked through the window and saw someone sitting in the corner behind the stove, all huddled up. I thought it was some bum. They come by here sometimes from the railroad, begging. Mom feeds them when Dad's not around. They leave signs for each other, you know. We never could see them but they must because they always come when Ma's alone or with me here. Anyway, I unlocked the door and went inside to see what sort of mess he might've made but he hadn't done anything.

'He woke when Tidy barked and right away said he was sorry, he'd leave right away and he seemed so terrified I felt sorry for him and said he should calm down. When he sat up I saw the liquor bottle there and knew he'd been drinking. He looked pretty awful, but I remembered seeing him in town and knew he'd had awful luck with his family and all. I asked if he had anything to eat and he said he didn't need anything. Well, I knew that was nonsense and I went back home and got bread, cheese and cold chicken and made a thermos of coffee and took it to him.'

Foote hadn't wanted to eat and was unwilling at first to sit at her desk where she laid out the food and poured coffee in a mug she'd brought. She finally coaxed him into her chair and, when he'd eaten, got him to talk about the children.

'Mostly he talked about Kitty when she was real small and affectionate. She'd sit in his lap and laugh at faces he made and sounds he'd work up. I imagine she turned to him because their mother spent more time with Buff, who was lots younger and needed the attention. Arthur said Kitty began to change when she started school. I hated to hear that—I like to think everything that happens in school is good for kids, but, of course, it's not always that way. Especially in bigger schools, where teachers can't keep an eye on everything. I guess you know there were stories about the Footes and kids would tease a girl like Kitty—'

I admitted I'd heard about that.

'Yes. And while it was hard for Kitty, she managed because she was a fighter, but it was much worse for Buff. Oh, he tried to fight, but being a boy and not fierce or big it was really tough. We were in the same class, you know. I saw a lot of it and heard about more. He pulled all up inside himself. Some kids said he was stuck up, but I thought he was just scared and shy.'

'Didn't he have any friends?'

'I don't remember any.'

'Was it different in high school?'

'Some. He could be real funny, you know, and was always making everybody laugh. He got into a little trouble with a few teachers because he'd say smarty things, but that just made him more popular with kids who didn't have his nerve.'

She didn't remember his being much involved with girls. When I asked if she knew he'd got close to an older woman she turned moderately pink.

'I suppose you mean Rose. That was after he graduated. There was talk, yes. I don't think it lasted long. He hung around Bond's a lot and he and Puck were pretty close there. Puck was always in the cafe those days and kidded with Rose and the three of them sat at the counter near the kitchen almost every night all that summer.'

'How'd you get Arthur out of your schoolhouse?'

'Oh, that was no problem. He kept saying he'd better go and I told him he should rest up all he wanted. I could tell he wanted to drink more but was ashamed to do it while I was there, so after a bit I said I had to get home and told him to stay on but keep the fire going so he wouldn't freeze. And then, all of a sudden, he told me I was an angel and he began to cry.'

The recollection choked her up and she lowered her head and was silent for several seconds, trying to get her voice back. Finally she lifted her head, smiled and carefully wiped her eyes with a little hanky she dug from her apron pocket. We both sat in silence while she put the hanky on the table and gently tried to press the wrinkles out.

The next morning there'd been no smoke

rising from the school chimney and Greta had hurried over to find Foote gone. He'd refilled the kindling box from the stack outside and had left no other signs except footprints in the snow.

I asked what her pa would've thought if he'd known Foote had been boozing in her schoolhouse and she'd brought him food.

She laughed. It was open and hearty, showing off small, baby-white teeth and transforming her blank face something wonderful.

'He wouldn't have understood any of it. It'd just absolutely bewilder him.'

'Would he get mad?'

'Dad? Come on, he's Norwegian. He never gets mad, he just gets confused and maybe annoyed. Eventually he accepts things. He doesn't approve, you know, but he accepts.'

'How do you think he'd feel about me being here with you?'

'Oh, he'd want to know why you'd come.'

'Is he a jealous man?'

She laughed again and shook her blonde head.

'When I was at the door, you said he wouldn't approve of you letting a man in when you were alone. I thought you were afraid he'd raise hell.'

She smiled shyly. 'I just said that because you made me nervous.'

'But you got over that?'

'Some.'

We smiled at each other. Then she stood up, walked to the stove, returned with the coffeepot and caught me looking her over. Her face turned pink as she lowered her eyes and carefully poured.

I started to ask where her folks were but decided that'd make her afraid I was trying to figure out how much time I had to make a move. The hell of it was, that's just the line my mind was taking.

'What made you decide you didn't have to be nervous?' I asked.

She placed the coffeepot back on the stove and turned to face me.

'You felt sorry for Arthur.'

'Why'd that matter?'

'You couldn't be real bad if you felt that way about him.'

I asked if she had a steady fellow and she said no. Yes, she'd gone to dances in Corden on Saturday nights a few times but hadn't enjoyed them too much. Most of the fellows were too shy or too bold and lots of them drank too much. I asked how she enjoyed teaching school and she said she loved it. There was nothing more fun than watching a little kid learn to read.

I finished my coffee, thanked her for it and her time and said I hoped I'd see her again soon. She didn't tell me to hurry back but nodded as if the notion didn't worry her any.

212

CHAPTER TWENTY

The wind had come up while I'd been inside, sharp enough to cut hope, colder than dead love. I lowered my head into it and hiked along the rutted snow. Before I reached the highway Christenson's Model T turned into the drive and I stepped out of the rut into the drifted snow as he pulled up beside me. He opened his door and squinted down. His wife peered around him.

'Lookin' for me?' he asked.

'Nope. Just dropped in on Greta for a cup of coffee.'

He thought about that for a moment.

'You could've got a cup easier at the cafe in town.'

'Wouldn't have been as good. Anyway, I wanted to talk with her about Buff Foote.'

'Why?' demanded Mrs. Christenson.

'I'm supposed to be investigating a murder.'

'You think he done it?'

That made Christenson blink and me shake my head.

'I'm just trying to learn all I can about everybody involved.'

'Well,' she said, jerking her head, 'Greta certainly wouldn't know anything about any of it.'

'Maybe not, but I got to ask. They were classmates, you know.'

The wind caught the car door and Christenson held on, then nodded at me, slammed it shut and drove on. I went back to town.

The lobby was warm, snug and empty except for Boswell, who was smoking his pipe in the rocker by the counter. I asked where everybody was as I stomped my feet and started unwrapping.

'Dining room. Playing cards.'

'Including the reverend?'

He nodded.

'You know if Johnstone tried to call his lawyer?'

'Uh-huh. Didn't get him. All steamed up about it.'

'That's reasonable. Why in hell wouldn't a man's lawyer be sitting by the telephone Saturday morning waiting for his client's call?'

Boswell, never one to make pointless talk, just looked serene and kept his pipe gurgling. I told him he was probably the only man in the world with a portable water pipe.

After a quick smoke I went in to talk with Elihu.

He was staring at the ceiling, probably waiting for the show to start when I entered; he rolled his head on the pillow to give me a blank look. I asked how he was.

'How do I look?'

'Like a man rehearsing for a coffin.'

He managed to raise his head an inch or so and peered down at the folded hands over his flat belly. He lifted the hands, regarded the hooked fingers a moment, then dropped his white head back on the pillow.

'Still dreaming?' I asked.

'Yeah. I'm off there more than here.'

'Where's it better?'

'There, I think. It seems all right to be mixed up in dreams. It's hell when you think you're awake but nothing's real. I hear another man's dead. How'd you let that happen?'

'I was in bed.'

'With Daisy?'

'No, not with Daisy, nor Bertha either. I got to sleep sometimes, old man.'

'The devil never sleeps.'

'That's the hell of it. How about God?'

He closed his eyes and thought that over.

'He rested, I remember—after making everything. I don't remember anything in the Bible after that where He rested or slept. Probably never had the chance. Or maybe, like me, He sleeps and dreams most the time. Maybe He don't care if school keeps or not anymore. Fed up with the lot of us.'

'You ever hear about Puck's being pals with Buff Foote?'

He blinked a couple times. 'Yeah.

215

Buff—that was Arthur's bastard boy, wasn't it?'

'More like Azalea's, but you've got the right idea.'

'Yeah, I remember. They hung out at Bond's. Both of 'em after that black-haired waitress, Rose.'

'Doesn't seem like that'd make them buddies.'

'It might, if neither got her.'

But one of them had. So what else would make them friends? Buff sure wasn't a hockey fan. Maybe they had a common enemy.

I told Elihu I'd see him later, grabbed my coat and went out into the cold. By then the sun had dropped below the west hill and the temperature had hit the skids.

Rose, Bond told me, had gone home with woman cramps. Puck hadn't been around all day. I went over to the pool hall and he wasn't there either.

It was too close to dinner for a visit with Abigail, so I went back to the hotel. Boswell still shared the lobby with the canary.

'Where's the gang?' I asked.

'Mostly still playing cards except your ma's in the kitchen and the reverend and his sidekick went upstairs.'

I went through the dining room and saw at a glance that O'Keefe was losing. That didn't surprise me. The eye-opener, though, was the sight of matches piled like a logjam in front of

216

the blushing bride, Mary Jane. Only she wasn't blushing, she was sitting there with a poker face and steady eyes. I got a grin from Kitty, but no one else noticed me.

Back in the kitchen Bertha told me Ma was feeding Elihu in the bedroom. I asked if Ma knew there was a poker game going on in her dining room.

'She knows,' said Bertha, 'but she don't let on.'

That was characteristic. Ma knew the crowd had to have something to do and as long as they didn't get loud or obvious she'd overlook indiscretions.

'You can tell them cardsharks to clear out and take the evidence off my tables,' Bertha told me. 'I'm about to serve supper.'

I passed on the news to the gambling crew and all but O'Keefe accepted it easily and even he only muttered a little as they settled up.

In the bedroom Ma was dabbing at Elihu's mouth with a napkin and he was jerking away as I came in.

'How's he doing?' I asked.

'His appetite's about as good as his temper is bad, so I guess he's fine. Where've you been all day?'

'I've been being a cop. That's the job I got that pays, you know?'

'Fine. In that case you'll be able to pay for your room and board.'

217

'Uh-huh. And who's gonna tend your fires and haul the groceries?'

She turned from the bed, folded her chubby hands in front of her middle and smiled serenely.

'Puck's agreed to handle all of that.'

Her smile broadened as my chin dropped.

'Yes,' she assured me, 'he dropped around this afternoon and when I complained that you were too busy to do your duties he offered to help out. He's a rough man, I know, but he has very fine instincts. Abigail recognized that when she let him come stay with her. Now he feels he may be compromising her by living there, so we've worked out an arrangement that I think will be very satisfactory all around.'

I glanced down at Elihu, whose hawk eyes held a sneaky glint.

I got my jaw back in joint, said it all sounded dandy and meandered back to the lobby. Gaylord and his man, Clint, had both arrived to be close for the dinner call and the reverend asked me how Elihu was doing.

I gave him Ma's diagnosis, which he accepted with a knowing smile. He asked me how my investigation was progressing.

'I'm glad you asked. You happen to know a man called Puck?'

As he raised his eyebrows I glanced past him at Clint, whose head had turned my way. His eyes looked thoughtful.

218

'No,' said the preacher. 'I assume that's a nickname.'

'Yeah. He grew up in your town, Aberdeen. Played hockey for Minnesota.'

'I'm afraid that means nothing to me. I've not kept up with sports.'

Just then the front door opened and Puck appeared with a battered suitcase and a rush of cold air. He gave me a gap-toothed grin, set the case on the floor and started pulling off his boots.

'Guess I ain't missed supper,' he said.

CHAPTER TWENTY-ONE

I half expected fireworks when Puck and O'Keefe met, but the only reaction I caught was a sly grin on Puck's kisser. I thought that was mighty Christian considering he'd had the worst of it when they'd tangled. On the other hand it was possible he was already planning how he'd settle accounts.

After supper I caught up with him in the hallway and nudged him into the parlor.

'Don't get any notions about settling O'Keefe's hash,' I warned him. 'One wrong move and your ass'll be back in the pokey.'

'Why, Carl,' he protested, 'a man like me don't ever go round getting back at fellas. You never got nowheres that way. And besides, your ma already warned me to watch my step.' He grinned. 'She don't miss a trick, huh?'

I rolled a smoke after we sat down and he looked so wistful I gave him my first one and rolled another. He took a deep drag contentedly and settled back into the easy chair.

'How'd you happen around here for a visit?' I asked.

'Well, I ain't been too busy, you know. And I got figuring you might need some help keeping the fire up and stuff. So I come in and asked about you, and that Daisy girl, she said you was out, but she got your ma and before I could make a offer she asked did I want work and I said sure thing. You ain't sore, are you?'

'Why'd I be sore?'

'Well,' he flapped one hand, 'it *was* your job and nobody said you'd quit yet. I come in just temporary, you know? When Joey's better he'll be cop again and you'll be back here taking care of things and I'll find something else.'

If he stayed sober it was possible I couldn't get the job back and, lousy as it was, it'd be galling to lose it to a guy who was a worse bum than me.

'I thought you and Abigail were getting cozy.'

'Oh, we got on fine. But she *is* a old maid

and they're persnickety. In that little house I couldn't loose a belch, let alone worse, without she'd hear and maybe faint.'

'You didn't have any trouble staying off the sauce?'

'Naw. It's easy when you're busted.'

We both knew he could always cadge a drink from Boswell's bottomless supply, but I guessed that'd be too much for his pride.

'I hear you and Buff used to be buddies. That right?'

'Well, yeah, we got on. Still do.'

'What'd you used to talk about at the cafe?'

He gave me a sly grin. 'Women mostly. Townfolk some.'

'Ever talk about his family?'

He took a long drag on his shrinking cigarette and squinted at the rising smoke.

'Not much. He talked about Kitty now and again. Thought the world of that girl. She raised him, you know. Not the ma or pa. It was her.'

'He ever talk about Arthur?'

He thought about that and finally shook his head. I asked if he had any notion why?

'Never thought about it. How much do you talk about your old man?'

He had me. I think about him plenty but don't remember ever jawing about him.

'Buff ever talk about the fire that killed his ma and the baby?'

'Yeah. Once. The first time he ever got

tight. He said it happened because old Arthur never had the chimney swept. He didn't go on a lot, you know, but you could tell it was on his mind bad. It made him real sour and that's not like him. Most the time he's all happy-go-lucky, telling stories and lies. He must know a million dirty stories. Like the one about the farm boy whose girl made him use a rubber and he didn't know enough to take it off after—'

I didn't think I wanted to hear about that one and asked if he'd ever heard Buff call Arthur his pa?

'No. Like I said, he didn't talk about him hardly ever, but when he did he just called him stuff like "that old fart."'

'You think he hated him?'

His smoke had burned down to within a finger width of his lip and he squinted at me as he carefully took it from his mouth.

'I don't figure he killed him, if that's what you're getting at.'

'I'm trying to figure out why he hated him—if he did. I keep thinking about this guy everybody tells me was harmless and I can't figure why he died so hard. Maybe his killer was just nuts, but I keep wondering . . .'

He tried to look thoughtful about that but didn't have the face for it and gave up.

'You never know,' he said.

He carefully butted out his cigarette on his shoe sole and dropped it into his pants cuff.

'You through with me?'

'No. You happen to know Arthur yourself?'

'Nope. Nobody knew him but maybe Boswell. He never talked to anybody else I know of. Never came by the pool hall or Bond's place. Strictly a loner.'

'How about Azalea?'

'No, she didn't hang out at any of those places either.'

I smiled to let him know I thought that was cute. He grinned back and propped his right ankle on his left knee to let me know he was perfectly happy to gab all night.

'You know Azalea when she lived in Aberdeen?'

'I wouldn't say so, no. I heard about her some. She went to the same grade school as me. Year or so ahead.'

'What'd you hear about her?'

'Oh, like she was a wildcat. Scrappy as hell and cute.'

'You never checked her out?'

'Hell, man, back in those days I was too busy playing hockey to mess with girls. Especially older ones.'

'Where'd you play?'

'In old man Jenson's back lot. He used to flood it every winter. Had it banked up on the sides, made a nice rink. And he bought us skates and sticks. Old Jenson was a Michigan man, you know, where they played lotsa hockey. Didn't have any kids of his own but he sort of adopted a flock of us. I was his favorite because I was the best on the ice. He all the time watched us and gave us tips. Even got on the ice some the first year there but he had a game leg and had to give it up. He lined things up for me at Minnesota. What he wanted was for me to go to Michigan, but he couldn't swing it there. If he'd have lived I'd probably finished school and done all right. But he died the beginning of my junior year. Everything kind of went to hell after that.'

'You found time for girls at Minnesota?'

'Yeah. I made the time, and a few other things.' He grinned.

'You flunked out.'

'Uh-huh. I was dumb.'

'Yeah, aren't we all?'

I rolled us each another smoke and we considered stupidity in silence for a while.

'You ever hear any stories about Azalea here in Corden?' I asked.

'What kinda stories?'

'Like that she went to the Cities every now and again to meet some guy.'

'No,' he shook his head, 'I don't remember hearing that.'

'You ever hear that Kitty and Buff weren't from Arthur?'

'Oh sure. I mean, hell, neither one of them took after him none.'

'Ever hear anybody blame Arthur for the

fire?'

'Oh sure. In this town somebody's always gonna blame somebody else for anything bad happening. 'Cording to them, there ain't no such thing as an accident.'

'You figure the fire was an accident?'

He looked at me thoughtfully for a moment before admitting he'd wondered some but concluded it didn't seem likely that it wasn't.

When we went back to the lobby Mary Jane and Kitty were rubbernecking out the east windows at all the cars and folks that'd moved into town for Saturday night. It was too cold for them to gather along the sidewalks as they did in summer, but there were as many cars parked diagonally at the curbs and horizontally along the crown of the main drag leaving two narrow lanes for those who were still wheeling around. In the summer old Joey always roamed up and down the street, making sure the cars parked tight and nobody blocked traffic. He didn't do that in the winter and neither did I, but everything seemed to go just as well. The brightest spot along the block east of the hotel was the theater with its million-bulbed marquee. Folks gathered under the lights like a mess of moths around a lantern.

'What's the place right across the street north of here?' I heard Mary Jane ask Kitty.

'That's the dance hall.'

'Really? They got a band and everything?'

'They have a band, more or less. I don't know about everything.'

'When does the dance start?'

'About nine the band begins and kids—little girls about ten—are let in and they dance until the crowd begins to show up. Then old man Lane, the owner, thumbs them out, and the paying customers take over.'

Mary Jane turned to Herb, who was sitting in a rocker near the hallway entrance looking bored.

'Let's go, Herb, I want to dance!'

'We won't know anybody.'

'We don't *need* to know anybody, silly. We'll dance with each other—come on!'

'How much is it?' Herb asked Kitty.

'A quarter for girls, fifty cents for guys.'

'I'll take you, Kitty,' said Buff.

'Okay—if I don't have to dance with you.'

'Herb'll dance with you,' offered Mary Jane. Herb looked a little spooked by that but didn't say no. She turned to me.

'You'll come, won't you?'

'Afraid not. Dancing's not my strong suit, and besides, I'm being a cop. Cops don't dance.'

'Oh pooh,' she said, and turned toward O'Keefe, who grinned evilly but turned to check with Johnstone, who was sitting beside him by the front door. Johnstone looked at Kitty, who ignored him. I could tell from his expression that he didn't want her to go. Not,

I guessed, because he feared local competition but because the crowd would be young and that would make him seem older and, worse, because he knew she was going as much to annoy him as to amuse herself.

He nodded at O'Keefe.

Mary Jane, in an excess of sociability by this time, invited Johnstone too. He gave her a kindly smile and said no thanks.

It was still too early to get into the Playhouse, so Buff suggested thay all go get a beer to put them in the right mood and suddenly the young folks were gone, leaving me with Boswell, Puck and Johnstone.

Johnstone said the building didn't look like a dance hall and I explained it was originally a repair garage but had been changed over a few years back when the town's first dance hall burned down. I started telling him more but could see he wasn't interested and let it drop.

Plant and his sidekick came in on time to end a deep silence. The preacher had been talking with Ma in the dining room and her respectful listening had him in a good mood. He smiled his benediction on us, asked where all the young folks had gone, smiled indulgently when I told him and settled down in the rocker directly across from me and next to Puck.

After a few casual remarks to Johnstone and a polite inquiry about my progress he rubbed his bald head and turned to his neighbor.

'I remember your face but am having trouble placing you. Didn't you once live in Aberdeen?'

'Yup.'

'I thought so. You repaired storm damage on our porch roof. Corner of Second and Fourth streets, right?'

'Could be, Reverend.'

Plant named the date, day and hour when Puck had arrived. Puck grinned and nodded. I figured it was the sort of showing off that comes easy since nobody's likely to challenge its accuracy.

'And your name's Johannes Olson, right?'

Puck gave me a sheepish look and nodded. No wonder he never went by anything but his nickname.

I asked how come he'd moved to Corden from Aberdeen. He said he'd been offered a job by old man Norris, who'd heard of him from a cousin in Aberdeen.

'Norris died way back, didn't he?' I asked Boswell. The old man stirred, took his stubby pipe from his mouth and said, yeah, mebbe a dozen years ago.

'Died a month after I went to work for him,' said Puck.

'So why'd you stay?'

'Got drunk and didn't have money to get back. One thing and another, just never made

228

it. Wasn't anything to go back to anyways.'

Plant lost interest in him and announced that he was going to visit Elihu. Clint went up to their room and Puck left for the pool hall.

I tried pumping Boswell about his recollections of Puck and he was willing to think about him but didn't have much to offer beyond saying he was a good customer any time he had money. I asked did he know if Puck ever hung around the Foote house and he couldn't help me on that. When he decided he might as well mosey back to his shack I put on my coat and hiked along with him. The sky had clouded over and the temperature was up above zero, so it felt almost balmy. Once he got his fire going and broke out his jug of moon, I wished him good night and left. As usual he said nothing about my turning down his offer of a snort; just nodded and poured his own.

I patrolled Main Street, dropping in on the pool hall and Bond's cafe. They were both crowded and noisy, full of smoke and good cheer.

It was around ten-thirty when I got to the dance hall. The music was thumping and the crowd was mostly having a big time. A coal furnace in the basement was pumping warm air up through the big register in the center of the hall between two iron poles that supported the ceiling, which was draped with dusty crepe paper decorations tacked up a

229

decade or so ago. The dancers moved in a counterclockwise direction around the heat. The six-man band occupied a little platform in the northeast corner and single girls flocked along the west wall while stags hung around the east side. There were chairs for the girls. The guys stood. Coats and jackets had been tossed over a railing that ran along the south side with a break toward the east where Eddie Ellis sat taking in money and putting a date stamp on the backs of customer hands. That way couples could go out and neck in their cars till they started to freeze and come back to thaw out. Single guys went out to get a drink since boozing wasn't allowed anywhere in the hall.

Eddie asked if I was planning to dance and I said, no, I just came around to see he didn't shortchange any customers. He said okay, but if he saw me dancing he'd call in the law.

I wandered in and on past where the girls were clustered but of course, neither Kitty nor Mary Jane were there. Both had probably never had a chance to sit down since they entered the front door. I caught glimpses of them. Kitty was with a tall dude I didn't recognize and Mary Jane was wrapped in O'Keefe's bear hug, beaming like a full moon. I didn't spot her faithful Hubby until I looked over the stag bunch and saw him standing at the edge of the crowd, looking lost. Buff was with a cute blonde.

The band was playing 'Darktown Strutter's Ball,' and the sax player, a skinny galoot with a carrot top, was singing, 'I'll be down to get you in a wheelbarrow, honey, 'cause a taxi costs too damned much money.' The stags snickered, the wallflowers looked properly shocked and the dancers were too busy to hear.

When the number ended the dancers broke up or wandered hand-in-hand off the floor. O'Keefe brought Mary Jane back to Hubby, who scowled at his bride while she tried to cheer him up without much success. Kitty came toward me with her tall dude trailing.

'Well,' she said, 'you going to dance with me?'

'Can't. Didn't pay.'

'So I'll buy you a ticket if you're too cheap.'

Her tall partner decided he was through and moved off after thanking her. She waved one hand without glancing his way.

'Kitty,' I said, bending toward her so she could hear me above the noise of the crowd, 'dancing's just a bum substitute for the real thing—'

'Baloney,' she said. 'When you do it right it's another part of the build-up and with a guy as fast as you are, there'd ought to be lots of that.'

I glanced around to see how many had caught that, but nobody was that interested.

'Okay,' I said, 'let's go back to the hotel and I'll take all the time you want.'

'Uh-uh, that's what you say now.'

She looked past me, smiling, and a couple guys moved in to say hi and start talking about high school days. She introduced them to me but we paid no attention to one another. I moved off and walked around, taking and giving smark cracks to guys who were friendly. I wandered past the west wall and saw O'Keefe giving the hustle to a couple girls who didn't look old enough to be out of high school yet. A couple stags edged in, scowling, and I guessed they had their own plans for the young ones. O'Keefe saw them from the corner of his eye and turned to measure them. One was his height and maybe even heavier. The other kid was stocky with the thick neck and big jaw of the Purvis clan, which was well known for its scrappiness. I eased in between the guys and O'Keefe and told him I had a message from Johnstone. He gave me a skeptical glance but apparently decided he couldn't take a chance that I was lying and followed me until we were apart from the crowd.

'Just a tip,' I said. 'You start messing with the kids and you could wind up with a mob on your back. Stick with Mary Jane and Kitty. You won't get anywhere, of course, but you won't get your ass fractured either.'

He shook his head.

'God, Wilcox, I don't know what I'd do without you—but I'd sure like to find out. Why don't you just go patrol your goddamn street.'

'I'm going to. And the fact is, I don't really give a shit what happens to you, but I've had to mess with two dead bodies this week and I'm not anxious for another. So pick on girls your own size and before long you'll be back in the big city sewers where you belong.'

He gave me a sneering salute that ended with his thumb on his nose and turned back to the wallflowers.

CHAPTER TWENTY-TWO

I strolled along the shoveled walk back to Bond's. The farm families had begun moving out and the stores were closing as the shoppers left. A good share of the remaining cars were steamed up by couples necking inside. I couldn't see the action but knew the smart ones would be snuggling in blankets and keeping their hands warm on each other while their feet turned to ice.

The cafe was filled with people, smoke and a steamy atmosphere. I elbowed my way along the counter, taking it slow and easy, and stopped at the south end where Dedee brought me black coffee and a quick, shy smile.

'Rose back?' I asked.

'Uh-huh. In the kitchen. She'll be out.'

I thanked her and looked around. A couple guys I'd known in school drifted by to make the usual smart remarks and moved on. It wasn't real obvious but I could feel a difference in their attitude since I'd become the town cop. They were uncomfortable because they were afraid their former familiarity made them vulnerable. It was as if I'd lived among them as a spy and had finally come into the open on the side of authority.

I was halfway through the coffee and a smoke when I saw Puck drift back to the men's room. A little while later the preacher's man, Clint, took the same route. I asked Dedee for a refill, rolled another cigarette and was well into it when Puck reappeared. A few seconds later Clint came out, glanced around casually, caught my eye and after a moment's hesitation nodded in agreement when I waved him my way.

'The reverend here with you?' I asked when he got to me.

He shook his head. 'He's up in his room, preparing a sermon.'

'He going to preach tomorrow?'

'He's been invited to address the Congregationalists.'

'My, my. That'll be quite a switch from their usual fare.'

234

'Yes,' he said with satisfaction. After a moment he gave me a side look with a short grin. 'I was instrumental in making the arrangements.'

'I bet you were. You're a great arranger. What were you working out with Puck in the men's?'

'Who?'

'Johannes Olson, the hockey player called Puck. The guy you just shared the can with.'

'Oh? So that's who it was. I didn't notice. He was inside and I was waiting outside. I didn't look at him.'

I stared at him and he looked back calmly. 'Who're you here with?' I asked.

'Mrs. Christenson and her daughter. They're in a booth near the entrance.'

'How do you like Greta?'

'She's a fine, Christian girl.'

'Uh-huh. You're not married, are you?'

'No.' He looked away, flushing a little.

'Never been?'

He looked me in the eye. 'My commitment has been to the Lord.'

'And the reverend. But he found time to marry.'

'That was before he recognized his true calling.'

'I see. You figure the true believer's got to be single, huh? That sounds kind of Catholic.'

'You're single, does that make you a

235

Catholic?'

I grinned at him and his fierceness disappeared in confusion as he realized the foolishness of his point.

'I've been married,' I said. 'Like most Catholics. And I've always found time for the ladies when they could find time for me. 'Course, I've never been as busy as you.'

'From what I've heard,' he said, looking past me, 'you've always found time for philandery.'

'If I couldn't find it, I'd make it. You find time to hear a lot, don't you? I'd guess one of your jobs is to keep track of people that interest the reverend. How'd you manage to keep in touch with the Foote family?'

Dedee approached to ask if he wanted anything and he shook his head at her and replied to me as she moved off.

'I don't spend my time in gossip and snooping. I heard about you quite inadvertently. A man of your notoriety is impossible to avoid. Now, I must get back to the Christensons—'

'Fine, I'll tag along. Want to talk with them anyway since gossip and snooping is my business these days. How long have you known Puck?'

He spoke as we shouldered our way through the citizenry.

'I don't know the man. I've seen him once or twice since we came here. That's all, and I don't think you have any right to intrude on the Christensons—'

'No intrusion,' I assured him. 'I know the ladies well.'

I got a fine smile from Greta as I slipped into the booth behind Clint and we sat facing the ladies. Mrs. Christenson was polite but looked bewildered when I told her Clint had invited me to join them for a few minutes. I glanced at him and he was trying to decide whether to call me a liar or not but chickened out when Greta said I was more than welcome.

I asked where her father was and she said he'd gone off with some friends. I tried to imagine what they'd be doing. He didn't play pool, drink beer, ogle girls or even talk much. I guessed he was maybe at the hardware store, admiring tools.

'How'd it happen,' I asked Mrs. Christenson, 'that the reverend's airplane landed in your field?'

'Oh,' she said, brightening up, 'we met him when we went to Aberdeen last year in the fall. We'd heard him preach over our neighbor's radio and I just made up my mind I had to see and hear him in person and we drove there and it was just wonderful. After the sermon I talked to him and later there was a picnic and we sat at his table and he was just as friendly and natural...'

She told me *all* about it.

237

Greta looked down at her cup through most of it but once or twice met my eye with a look that asked for tolerance. I gave her my most innocent smile and she returned it in a better wrapper.

Finally Clint coughed gently with his hand over his mouth and Mrs. Christenson hushed abruptly and turned his way.

'Excuse me,' he said. 'I think I should get back to the reverend. He rather likes to try out parts of his sermons on me and by now I suspect he's finished.'

Mrs. Christenson apologized for talking so much and said how wonderful it must be to have the confidence of such a man as the reverend and to be able to share in his work and his mission.

Clint managed to look modest and proud all at once and I let him out so he could bow. I thought he was going to kiss Greta'a hand but he only gestured her way and backed into a farmer as he started off.

Greta giggled when he was out of sight and her mother gave her an elbow and then put both hands on the table before her and asked me straight out if Mr. Cogswell was helping me with my investigation of the murders. I was so startled it took me a couple seconds to remember that Cogswell was Clint's last name.

'What made you think that?' I asked her.

'Well,' she waved her pudgy hand, 'I only

thought that you were just interested in that. It's why you came out to the farm and why you talked with Greta, isn't it? And he's a very intelligent man. I'd think he would be a great help in any serious matter.'

'Yeah, I guess he would if he was of a mind to. Did he just happen by you in here?'

'Well, not exactly *happen*. The day they arrived in their airship he asked if we'd be in town Saturday night and I said of course we would and he asked what we did and I told him we shopped and then stopped in here and he said, well, maybe he'd drop by and he did.'

'You think maybe Greta caught his eye?'

She laughed, glanced at her blushing daughter and laughed again. 'He may have been attracted, why not?'

'A man'd hardly be a man if he weren't,' I said.

Mrs. Christenson liked the sentiment but wasn't too pleased with its coming from me and turned toward the door, muttering something about her husband showing up soon. Greta gave me another warm smile.

I decided to quit while ahead, wished them good evening and moved out.

The wind was picking up and the few citizens still around were tucking their chins into coat collars and pulling scarves tight as I headed for the dance hall.

It was hot and loud inside and the mob

239

dancing was dense enough that I had trouble finding Kitty. When the dance number ended she drifted my way with about four guys trailing along. I offered to take her away from all this and she said fine, she needed a beer.

We grabbed a table in the center of the beer parlor just as a couple got up and for a few minutes I was busy spooking off the kidders and stags.

When we were finally alone I asked if Arthur had ever made a pass at her.

She frowned and said that wasn't even funny.

'He had no more sex drive than a rock.'

'Yeah, but he was affectionate, wasn't he?'

'Oh sure. He loved it when I hugged him or Ma rubbed his shoulders or kind of mussed his hair. And I could tell he wanted to hug Buff sometimes, especially when he was little and cute. Anybody'd want to hug Buff. He was like a little old teddy bear.'

'You sure the old man never did hug him?'

'You're getting at something,' she said.

'Somebody sent Arthur a letter not long before he was killed. It called him a pervert. What do you figure was at the bottom of that?'

'Some nut with a poison pen. Those kind of people don't have to know anything, they just try to make people feel awful.'

'This wasn't just a poison pen job. It was a threat and it came from somebody who hated

240

his guts. Why'd anybody hate him like that?'

She thought about that, drank some beer, wiped her mouth delicately and glanced around the crowded room.

'It might've been somebody that hated him because he got to marry Ma.'

'Like who?'

'Well, how about the Reverend Plant? Or his man Clint? Maybe even Puck.'

'How about Buff?'

'Come on, Carl, that's crazy. He's scared to death of blood. When we were kids he bloodied my nose once and went into a screaming panic.'

I figured what scared him was what he expected she'd do to him but I let it ride.

'Okay. So why'd you mention Puck?'

'Well, he had a case on her. Always hung around. He pretended he was nuts about Buff and I think he really did like him, but he always got calf-eyed when he looked at Ma.'

'How'd she take that?'

'She liked it. She was never moony or anything but he gave her a lift and she made sour cream cupcakes for him and coffee. She made him pay up by hauling our garbage out and helping her with the dishes.'

'How'd Arthur go for that?'

'Puck never showed up when he was around. You know, I never thought about that back then. Maybe I didn't want to. I just enjoyed seeing Ma feel good.'

241

'How'd Puck treat you?'

'Real careful. Never touched me.'

I asked if her ma had ever asked her to go outside and play when Puck was around and she shook her head.

'Maybe that's why I never suspected anything. And anyway, I just expected everybody to love Ma. It seemed right and natural.'

She looked at her watch and up at me.

'We going to dance together tonight? It's getting late.'

'I'd rather dance after the hall closes.'

'There won't be any music.'

'You can hum.'

She shook her head. 'It's now or never.'

So we went back to the dance hall.

CHAPTER TWENTY-THREE

Ellis gaped when I handed him my fifty cents, and he forgot to stamp the back of my hand. It was traditional for the town cop to show up for the last dance, not because he had to make the place close before the pumpkin hour but so as to take the blame off the band and hall owner in the eyes of the crowd. It wasn't traditional for the cop to dance.

The music was slow and the floor crowded so all we could do was hug and sway. At first

I kept thinking of more questions I wanted to ask Kitty but when I started to speak she pressed her cheek against mine and said romantically, 'Shut up.'

Pretty soon all I could think about was getting her back to the hotel and into bed.

Then the band began playing 'Good Night Ladies.'

'Well, hell,' said Kitty.

We danced it through and then shuffled with everybody else toward the piled coats while the bandleader kept calling 'Good night.' I helped Kitty into her wrap and she held my hand as we walked out into the cold. After a couple of steps she leaned into me and said, 'I can't do it tonight.'

I managed to say okay without growling. When I didn't look at her she stopped, reached up and turned my face to hers until we were staring at each other through fluffy snowflakes. When one landed on my nose she brushed it off with her gloved hand.

'Are you sore?'

'I'm gonna be.'

'It won't be fatal.'

'Why'd you wait till now to tell me?'

'I wanted us to dance. If you'd known, you wouldn't have.'

A passing smartass suggested I put the cuffs on her and I turned to glare at his back. Kitty touched my face again.

'We could still talk,' she said. 'That's what

you wanted a while ago.'

It sounded painful but I started remembering the questions I'd had in mind and said okay. She gave me a smile that should have brought on spring and said, 'You won't be sorry.'

The lobby was dark except for the counter light and all the rockers were empty. We climbed the stairs and I made a pass down the hall past Johnstone's room before returning to Kitty's door.

'His light's out,' I told her.

'Good,' she said. The room was dark and she had moved to the far side of her bed. I could hear the rustle of her clothes and my hopes and inspiration began to rise.

The bed creaked faintly as she settled down and I moved over, slipped off my shoes and sat on the edge.

'We're just going to talk,' she said.

My hopes drooped.

'No touch?'

'You can hold me but there's no point in exploring—you're not going anyplace and, besides, you've covered all the territory before—'

'Yeah, but I'm not tired of it—'

'Well just cut it out. What'd you want to talk about?'

I settled on my back, tucked a pillow under my head and said I wanted to know all about the night of the fire.

'I don't want to talk about that. I already told you that.'

'I've got to know about it.'

She was quiet for a few seconds, then rolled toward me, felt for my face and moved down until I could feel her warm breath.

'Kiss me. A nice quiet one, like I was somebody you give a damn about.'

I did and after a little while she pulled away, wriggled around until we were fitted together like spoons and held on to my left hand just under her breast.

'Ma left on a Friday morning. It was the first week of August, I think, maybe the second. She'd decided real sudden—I'm not even sure of the excuse she gave, I think she claimed a cousin was bad sick in Chicago and it was an emergency. She was all excited, that I remember. She chattered and promised to bring us all presents when she came home—'

'How'd Arthur react?' I asked, trying to pull my hand loose. She hung on.

'He was sad and quiet. Of course he was usually quiet but this time he was absolutely dumb. She didn't say anything *to* him, if you know what I mean, she just prattled on—'

'How old was she then?'

'I'm not sure—early thirties—anyway she took off saying she'd be back sometime the next week, probably no sooner than Tuesday, maybe later. She told me to get Miz Hendrickson to come over and babysit on

Saturday because she knew I'd be at the dance and she couldn't depend on Buff or Arthur.'

'She knew he went on a drunk when she left town?'

'Well sure, all of us did. Come on, relax, will you?'

I'd tried to get my hand free again and she hung on, so I quit the struggle and tried to think of something besides her hot body.

'What was the weather like?'

'Saturday there was rain in the afternoon and it stayed cloudy through sunset so it was fairly cool for August. It was real comfortable in the dance hall.'

'When'd you hear about the fire?'

She was silent for a moment and I tensed up when I heard a creak in the hall but it wasn't repeated and I guessed it was only caused by the wind.

'It was getting on toward midnight,' she whispered. 'I was dancing with the Scott boy and he was awkward and so excited it was embarrassing. He was trying to get closer and I was holding him off and when the number ended—they were playing "Marie"—he was trying to talk me into another dance and I was looking around for help and saw Joey by the front entrance with a lot of people and someone pointing at me and then he was hurrying me out saying there'd been a fire and I thought, no, it couldn't be our house, old Miz Hendrickson didn't smoke and she'd not be cooking—all that went through my head while at the same time I knew Joey wouldn't be mistaken about something like what was happening. Then we were at the house and it was all burning—you could see the skeleton sort of—you know? The two-by-fours showed through—and the next thing I saw Miz Hendrickson and asked her where was the baby and she cried and said it's with *her* and I said her who and she said your mother and I asked where and she pointed at the house.'

She lost her voice and I pulled her closer and got my hand free and brought it up to her face. Her cheek was wet. She took a deep breath and her voice became a little stronger.

'I got mad. I said it couldn't be Ma, she was with her lover, hundreds of miles away and Miz Hendrickson shook her head and cried some more and said, no, she'd come home on the eight-o'clock and had gone to bed upstairs with the baby.'

Her voice petered out once more and we were both silent while I felt her breathing and pulled her warmth against me. And pretty soon I realized that for the first time in my life I was in bed with a woman I'd not just made love to and didn't have a hard-on.

'Mrs. Arhart came around and took me to her house,' said Kitty. 'I didn't see Arthur until I'd been there awhile and still later Joey brought Buff in. He looked like a little old man. Arthur smelled drunk and couldn't talk. When he tried to, he choked.'

'Where'd he been?' I asked.

'He never said.'

'Didn't anybody wonder how come there was a fire in the fireplace in August?'

'Arthur said it was something Ma did when she felt blue. She liked to sit and watch it and rock the baby.'

'But if she was watching it, how come she was upstairs when the chimney caught fire?'

'She must've got tired and gone up to bed.'

I didn't comment on that and kept stroking her cheek until suddenly she twisted around, kissed me hard, pulled away and said I'd better go.

'I've gotta know one thing more,' I said.

'What?'

'I want to know what happened when she came home the time before.'

She turned her back once more and after a few seconds began talking.

CHAPTER TWENTY-FOUR

While she talked I heard the younger guests returning and tried to keep track while I listened. Pretty soon they'd all gone to their own rooms and by then Kitty was talked out

248

and sleeping quietly. When I finally slipped away she muttered sleepily and stirred but didn't wake.

I stood by the door listening awhile, heard nothing but the wind and moved into the hall. My mind was too busy for sleep and I went down to the lobby, rolled a smoke, lit up and stood by the window north of the front door.

The floor creaked behind me and I turned to see Puck ease out of the parlor. It was too dark to see him clearly but I caught sight of his gap teeth so he must have been grinning.

'You don't sleep much,' he said softly.

'I suppose,' I said, 'that mostly you call him.'

He came a little closer and I could see his eyebrows rise.

'If he called you, it would've been more noticeable. Somebody would've wondered.'

'Got another smoke?' he asked.

I took out my tobacco bag and papers and handed them over.

'I checked your room a while back,' he said. 'You wasn't there.'

'I know.'

'I guess you was talking with Kitty.'

'That worry you?'

He was clumsy with the tobacco bag and spilled some as he tried to pour the paper full. I took the bag back and watched as he rolled the cigarette and twisted the ends. I handed him my butt for a light and after a long drag he backed up and sat down in a rocker.

'You got a great way with the ladies,' he told me. 'I always wondered how you did it.'

'Okay, I'll explain it to you if you'll tell me how you managed with Azalea.'

He let out smoke and shook his head behind the thin cloud.

'I never, what you call, managed with her. I was fond, I won't lie about that—'

'Kitty heard you two that night. The time she went to the reverend, next to the last time. She came back early then too. So how'd you know she'd be home that night?'

'I kept an eye on the place, that's all.'

'Uh-huh. How come you weren't watching the night the house burned?'

He bent forward and rested his forearms across his knees.

'Jesus, if you knew how many times I asked myself that—'

'The baby *was* yours, wasn't it?'

'Yeah, it was.' He lifted his head enough to glare at me. 'So what?'

'Did you plant it for fun or on orders?'

He twitched and I began to lean forward, expecting him to jump, but he only straightened up and rested his hands on the flat chair arms.

'I don't know what you're talking about.'

'Sure you do. Clint, the reverend's dogboy, called you, or maybe you called him, just part

250

of the routine, keeping in touch. I figure the reverend was busy with his sick wife when Azalea got to town and his conscience took over so he couldn't meet her and sent Clint to manage things. And Clint told her it was all over and she'd best go home and tend to her family so she got back to find her old pal Puck all full of sweet sympathy and one thing led to another, including the baby. Right?'

'Clint didn't have nothing to do with nothing,' he said and tilted the rocker back. 'Yeah, I did come around when she came home. It was just pure luck. I was always keeping an eye on the place. A man'll do that when he's caught like I was. You get a feeling about somebody like Azalea. I just knew when she was around, nobody had to call me.'

'How about the next time, after the baby? Where were you then?'

'I was drunk, that's where I was. If I hadn't been, she'd still be alive.'

'Puck, old buddy, you're a goddamned liar. I know you kept in touch. I've talked with Kitty and Clint and I *know*.'

'Bullshit. Clint wouldn't never tell you anything and Kitty never knew—'

He stopped as I grinned at him and stared back. Then he carefully butted out his cigarette on his right heel and got up.

'I'm gonna bank the fires down and go to bed. You want to spin any more tales, come

251

along.'

I said dandy and followed him down the dark hall, around the corner of the main dining room through the private room and down the narrow, dark stairs to the cellar. He lit the light at the foot of the stairs and walked across the dirt floor, turned on the second light, a naked bulb dangling from the low ceiling before the furnace. When he opened the iron door red light reflected on his ruddy face, turning it into a devil's mask as he grimaced.

The cellar smelled of dry earth and drier heat and just a hint of old apples from the fruit bins in the south corner.

Puck bent toward the galvanized clinker tub and picked up the iron tongs.

'I don't figure,' I said, 'that you came to Corden on Clint's orders. It was probably just luck for him that you got a job here about the same time Arthur and Azalea moved. But he heard about it and knew you'd need money and got in touch pretty quick. Because all the time he was worrying about how this business with her could ruin the reverend and his whole life.'

Puck hefted the tongs, looked into the fire pit, reached in and poked around, trying to get hold of a clinker near the center.

I leaned against a four-by-four ceiling support about two yards from the furnace and started rolling a smoke.

'I'm still not sure why Arthur got killed. Especially after Azalea was gone. Now her killing, that had to be you or Buff. If it was him, of course it was an accident—he was trying to get Arthur and didn't know his ma was back and upstairs with the baby. That's the kind of thing a crazy kid might do.'

Puck concentrated on working the clinker free, pulled it slowly toward the furnace door, hooked it on the frame and lost it. His jaw muscles flexed and sweat beaded his flattened nose.

'There could've been two reasons for you to start the fire. First because you were nuts about her and when she came back from the preacher meeting she was only home to get her baby and go back with him permanent and you couldn't stand the notion. Or maybe you weren't all that romantic and Clint had told you to stop her from going back. I'd kind of like to take the first notion but figure the second's more real.'

I might as well have been talking to myself. Puck wrestled the clinker out of the furnace, dumped it in the tub, put the tongs down and reached for the poker. I inched back so I could dodge behind the four-by-four.

'Arthur must've been quite a burden for Clint,' I said. 'After Azalea was gone he started turning weird, drinking more, doing crazy things like chasing kids off a lot he didn't own anymore, living like a hermit.

253

And when he found out Buff hated the navy and was in trouble, he got this notion that the great father, Gaylord Plant, could make everything right, and he decided to get in touch. And I figure he tried through you.'

Puck shoved coals around with the poker, put it down, got the shovel and pitched in coal. Then he slammed the iron door shut with the shovel edge and leaned the shovel against the wall.

I stood aside as he pulled the light cord and walked past me toward the stairs. He let me turn out the stair light, hiked down the hall, got his jacket and slipped it on. I followed suit and we went back through the dark kitchen and the shed, stepped into the snow out back and hiked, single file, toward the west wing cellar.

The sky was overcast, but the white snow and hotel seemed to make the earth glow enough to cast shadows, though there were none. All of the windows looking down on us were dark.

The cellar doors creaked enough to echo as Puck pulled them open and laid them back. We went down into the darkness, he opened the inner door, hit the switch just inside and headed for the boiler. Once more he opened the iron furnace door and glared into the red glow. He stopped sweating during our walk but wiped his face with his sleeve anyway and reached for the poker.

I caught his swing with the shovel snatched from its place against the wall, ducked his second blow and caught him in the chest with the shovel haft as I charged and slammed him against the furnace. He grunted, twisted, wheeled away and tried to turn back as I pushed the shovel up toward his throat. He jerked away, doubled up, hit the floor, rolled and came up in a crouch. I stayed with him and caught his jaw with my left elbow, got my right hand behind his knee, stood straight and dropped him head down and ass up. It stunned him enough that I had time to snatch up the poker he'd dropped and when he rose I broke his arm a little below the right elbow.

He moaned, clutched the break with his left hand and lay quietly on his side.

'Was it you or Buff that killed Arthur?' I asked as I crouched over him.

He told me to do what I couldn't or wouldn't.

'Okay, what I really want to know is, which reason did you burn Azalea for?'

He shook his head and repeated himself.

'Okay. I'm going after the doc. If you get up and leave here, I'll break both your legs when I catch you—and I'll catch you.'

CHAPTER TWENTY-FIVE

Doc congratulated me on causing a reasonably clean break as he worked on Puck in the City Hall cell. His patient wasn't that gushy about it and didn't even thank me when I handed him my emergency pint before locking him in.

As we walked back east I told Doc I hoped he was grateful that this time he didn't have to examine a corpse in the cold.

'You got me out of bed.'

I couldn't make a debate out of that but said that as long as he was up how'd he like to do me another favor.

'This one you won't get paid for,' I assured him.

We were almost to the hotel door by then and he stopped and looked up at me. His goatee and mustache looked phonier and blacker than ever in the snow light and his dark eyes squinted suspiciously. He's got no more sense of humor than a cat but he's one of the few men in Corden shorter than me so I like him anyway.

'Just what,' he said, 'do you have in mind?'

'I'm gonna have to talk with Buff and I want a witness.'

'Tonight?'

'Yeah. Before he finds out about what

happened with Puck.'

He stared at me for a moment, then looked around as if trying to convince himself he was standing on Main Street at 2:00 A.M. talking to a madman.

'You expect him to be violent?'

'Probably not, if I catch him in bed.'

He sighed, shifted his shoulders and said lead on.

We left our coats and his bag in the downstairs hall and went up to Buff's room. I didn't knock, just stepped inside, raised my hands with touching thumbs, brushed the light cord and jerked it on.

Buff's room was a little bigger than mine with a three-quarter bed in the northwest corner, one window overlooking the balcony on Main and a woven rag rug ugly enough for a rest home.

He was way down in that drugged sleep that comes the first hour after a man hits the sack when he's full of booze. He couldn't face the light or make any sense of our presence for several minutes. He kept saying, 'Lemme sleep, lemme alone...'

'Sure,' I said, 'right after you answer a couple questions, okay?'

'Too tired,' he moaned, 'go on—'

'What'd Arthur do to Kitty?' I asked.

'Raped her—go on, lemme sleep.'

'How'd you find out?'

'Puck knew—tol' me—'

257

'How'd Puck know that?'

He tried to bury his head under the pillow. I reached over, grabbed the corner and tugged. For a couple seconds he tried to hang on, then let go and rolled toward the wall.

'Just tell me and you can sleep,' I told him. 'Was it Clint that told Puck what happened?'

'Clint knows everything—'

'Including how to handle people. How'd he get you to kill Arthur?'

He stopped breathing and became rigid.

'Kitty never told you he raped her, did she?' I asked.

He rolled back toward me, got his feet on the floor and started forward.

'Gonna be sick . . .' he said.

I stepped aside and he stumbled past and down the hall with me close behind. The next moment he was on his knees before the toilet. It was awesome. I figure he got rid of just about everything but his tailbone. He used about half a roll of toilet paper to mop up his chin. I flushed away his offering and stood by while he waited for more.

'You think he'll survive?' I asked Doc, who had followed us down the hall.

'It's likely,' he said. The diagnosis didn't seem to cheer up the doctor any more than the patient.

Buff tried a couple more times to bring up the tailbone and then let me lead him back to his room.

'How about it,' I said as he collapsed back on his bed, 'Kitty didn't tell you about any rape, did she?'

'She told me about that Plant guy—'

'Gregory?'

'I don't wanna talk anymore. Leave me alone.'

'As soon as I get things straight. Kitty didn't tell you Arthur raped her, did she?'

'No.'

'All right. You want to know why Doc's here?'

He didn't answer but curled up like a baby.

'He had to set Puck's arm. Puck and I had a little fracas in the west cellar. He told me you set the fire that burned up your ma and the baby.'

He thought about that a few seconds before peeking up at me.

'He tell you that right after you broke his arm?'

'No, not until I threatened to break the other one.'

He straightened, rolled onto his back and folded his arms over his head.

'He said you figured it was Arthur up there because you thought your ma was still gone. So you loaded up the fireplace, doused it in kerosene and threw in a match.'

'Puck didn't tell you that,' he said in a faraway voice. 'He wouldn't tell a thing like that if you broke everything including his

259

balls. It was Arthur that set that fire. He found out she was going to take the baby and leave, just go off with that Jesus man and never come back. He did it to purify her.'

For several seconds there wasn't a sound in the room but our breathing. Doc finally cleared his throat but said nothing.

'Okay,' I said. 'You're doing fine. You found that out when you beat the old man before hanging him, right?'

'Yeah. But I didn't hang him. That was Puck's idea. I didn't care by then, I was too tired.'

'Which one of you killed Gregory?'

'That was Puck too. I just led him up there and he got him quick. The poor sucker never knew what hit him.'

'Okay,' I said. 'You've unloaded it all. Go to sleep.'

As I started to close the door behind me, Buff called out.

'You know the last thing he said?'

'Who?'

'Arthur. He said he deserved it. And he said he loved me. The old bastard knew what that'd do.'

As we went down the hall I told Doc maybe he'd ought to have given him something to make him sleep.

Doc scowled at me and said, 'Let him sweat.'

It seemed like murder brought out the best

260

in all of us.

CHAPTER TWENTY-SIX

I'd heard the church bells ringing for a while but that wasn't what woke me. It was Daisy, knocking timidly at the door, saying Puck was missing and somebody had to do the fires because it was forty below and everything'd freeze if I didn't get to it.

So I scrambled and when both furnaces were roaring, dragged myself back to the kitchen just in time to be told Elihu was coming to breakfast and I should go help him to the table. He didn't thank me, all he did was lean hard and bitch steady. At the table he took his place and glared around at the strangers. Ma had decided, in honor of the occasion, that we'd sit around the big banquet table and she introduced all the guests who hadn't seen Elihu before. His fierce eyes put a damper on the conversation for a while but pretty soon Bertha's pancakes, bacon and coffee mellowed things and there was some polite conversatiom.

I butted in on Johnstone to ask Kitty if by any chance she'd seen Buff this morning? She shook her dark head.

I finished my coffee, went up to Buff's room and looked inside. He wasn't there or in the toilet or shower. I went downstairs and saw his pea jacket and wool cap on the peg where he'd left them the night before. A quick inventory of the other coats didn't show up anything missing that I could remember.

In the kitchen Bertha told me, no, she hadn't seen him and neither had Daisy. I went out and took another look at the thermometer, which had warmed to only minus thirty-eight. The ground was covered with about two inches of fresh powder snow and the air was so still it didn't stir.

I got into my coat and knit cap, wrapped Elihu's wool scarf around my neck and lower face and stepped out the front door. The only tracks in sight led south. I followed them.

He'd walked the first couple blocks and then started to run. The light snow had scattered under his feet, making weird, almost shapeless tracks. The sky was frozen blue, the sun blinding and low behind me. My shadow stretched ahead so far it must've reached the north pole.

A little beyond the city limits he'd stumbled and fallen to his hands and knees but had kept on going, still trying to run but obviously in trouble.

Frost built up along the scarf under my nose and my hands grew stiff with cold inside my sheep-lined mitts.

By the time he'd reached the cemetery gates he'd slowed to a staggering walk.

I found him curled up, much the way he'd been the night before when I questioned him on his bed. His only cover were the pajamas he'd been wearing and his black shoes. His arms were folded tight against his chest, his white face touched the snow and there was frost around his nose and mouth.

Well, shit, I thought again, and started back at a dogtrot, heading for the sun.

CHAPTER TWENTY-SEVEN

By the time Doc and I got back out there in his Buick and I returned to the hotel, everyone but Elihu, Bertha and Daisy had gone to church.

Elihu was sitting in the parlor with a blanket around his legs and the Sunday paper in his lap.

'Well,' he said, 'I might've known you didn't go to church. Where the hell you been?'

I sat down across from him and rolled a smoke.

'It was such a nice day, I took a stroll to the cemetery.'

He ignored that and asked where was Puck?

'In jail.'

'What'd he do, get drunk again?'

'No. He killed a man.'

'Must've been drunk.'

'He might've been. He killed the preacher's son. Gregory.'

He thought that over, told me to get him a cigar and was slumped back with his eyes closed when I returned. The blue eyes came to life as I handed over the cigar.

'Why'd Puck kill Gregory?' he asked as he twisted off the cigar wrapper.

'I think he did it for the preacher's sidekick, Clint Cogswell.'

'Why'd that be a favor to him?'

'Well, Gregory was a reporter and he was bitter against his pa. I figure Clint saw big problems if this kid was able to dig up something about the connection between Arthur's murder and the preacher's little escapade with Azalea some years back.'

He wanted to know what that was all about and I told him.

When I was through he tapped his cigar ash into the tray on the table by his elbow and rolled the cigar gently between his stained fingers.

'It sounds like a mess,' he told me. 'What about Puck, you saying he's been a flunky for the reverend's man all these years?'

'Seems like.'

'So, you freezing him over at City Hall?'

'No. Ernie keeps up the fire there.'

'And feeds him?'

264

'No. I'm just about to do that. If Bertha'll cooperate.'

'So tell her I sent you,' he said and I did and she made a good breakfast and Daisy carried it covered with a couple of towels while I led the way and opened doors.

Puck looked rough what with his whiskery face and arm in a sling but he gave Daisy a rueful grin when she placed the tray on his bunk and lifted off the towels.

'I've about got it all,' I said after Daisy'd left and he was into the scrambled eggs, bacon and coffee. 'Buff unloaded last night. He told me he beat Arthur and you hanged him and later did in Gregory and that old Arthur set the fire that killed Azalea and the baby.'

Puck lowered his fork and stared at me.

'Now why the hell'd Buff tell you that?'

'He was drunk and sleepy and I kept him awake. He was also up to his eyebrows in guilt. It was so bad that after he unloaded to me and Doc, he took a walk to the cemetery without a coat and froze to death.'

'No.'

'Oh yeah.'

He swallowed hard, put his fork on the plate and leaned back against the brick wall.

'Come on, you're shittin' me, aren't you?'

'No, I'm not. He died on his ma's grave.'

He shook his head, not wanting to believe it.

'What boils me is that Clint's the son of a bitch behind all of it, and he's gonna come off free as a hawk.'

Puck looked around the cell, glanced down at his unfinished breakfast and slowly picked up the coffee cup and sipped. Then he held it in both hands and leaned forward, staring at the floor.

'Of course it might've all come from the preacher himself,' I said.

His eyes lost a little of their blankness and he squinted at me.

'Well,' he said, 'which one of 'em you want to pin?'

'Whoever caused it all.'

'Shit, man, who are you trying to kid? How the hell you gonna figure who caused it? It could've been Azalea—she made the play for the preacher at the start, it could've been the preacher, he went for her, it could've been old Clint trying to save his savior. That dumb turd thinks Plant is God or at least the goddamned engineer on his gravy train and he'd work the whole race to keep it on the track—'

'That's how I see it. Clint headed Azalea off the last time she came to see Plant. Told her it was over and sent her back to you for the second time, right?'

'Naw. The first time Buff was the one told me she was home early and alone. She'd showed up sudden and sent old lady

266

Hendrickson home and was crying and carrying on so Buff was scared and he came after me. I got him settled down upstairs—'

'Where was Kitty?'

'Sleeping up there. She was a great sleeper, that kid.'

'So what'd Azalea tell you?'

'She said the preacher's wife was sick and going to die and when she did, then the preacher'd be able to marry her, Azalea, and she'd have him to herself but she'd go to hell because she had prayed for the wife to die and she'd be damned for it. And she asked me to make a fire for her—it wasn't cold but she had a chill—so I fixed that up and sat beside her and when she cried I held her and then I went crazy and did it to her right there on her couch with both kids sleepin' upstairs.'

'Didn't she fight?'

'Oh yeah, she tried to stop me, but not hard. I mean, she was the kind of woman knows how a man is and blames herself when he gets started. She cried but she didn't go wild with the claws and biting. And afterward, when I told her I was sorry, she never blamed me none. She said I couldn't help myself. And I couldn't. If she'd've screamed or fought so hard I'd hadda hurt her to do it, I'd have stopped. But she just gave in—'

'What about the second time she came back early?'

'Well, that time Clint called, yeah. He'd get me through the speakeasy. Through Clyde, him that runs the beer parlor now. He'd let me know and I'd call back collect. He'd got it out of her that I'd got her pregnant before and he told me she was upset and needed me. This time there wasn't anybody there but Azalea and the baby. She'd sent old lady Hendrickson home again but this time she kept the baby in her arms and wouldn't let me touch her. I made a fire like the time before and she told me it was all over between her and the preacher. He thought he'd talked with God and he knew if he kept carrying on with Azalea he'd fry in hell and he passed on the word through Clint that she'd ought to repent and be saved and she said she was going to do that and she'd pray for me and I should go. The last I seen of her she was going up them stairs, carrying the baby that was mine.'

'So you built the fire into a roarer and left her to burn.'

'No, I never. When I walked out the fire was burning quiet and steady. Old Arthur came back and done it, that's who. He was coming up to the door when I left. He didn't say nothing to me and I didn't say nothing to him. He 'fessed up to it all when Buff went after him in the shed—'

'The way you guys beat up that poor old man before you hung him, he'd have

268

confessed to crucifying Christ.'

'Mebbe so, but he done it all right. That's the only way it could've happened.'

He hunched over his half cup of coffee while I leaned against the bars by the door and looked through the high window at the bright blue sky beyond the south wall. Finally I studied Puck once more.

'So all that happened ten years ago. What got Buff all fired up at this stage?'

'Oh hell, it's all mixed up. When Buff didn't like the navy old Arthur started calling the preacher. See, he figured that with all his money and friends, he could do something to get Buff out, like in Civil War days when people could buy their way out of service, you know? Clint got the calls and tried to stall him off and all but he got more and more troublesome and when Buff got into some trouble about hitting an officer, Arthur went nuts and said to Clint it'd be pretty awful if folks found out the son of the great preacher was going to prison. That got Clint all shook up and finally he went to see Buff at a navy base there by San Francisco or someplace and Buff got drunk right after and went AWOL and showed up here.'

I thought about that awhile and said I guessed Puck had told Clint about seeing Arthur enter the house the night of the fire. He admitted he had.

'So he had you kill Gregory because he was

a reporter and was nosing around for a story connecting the preacher with Arthur?'

'It wasn't like that at all,' he said as he put his cup on the breakfast tray and leaned once more against the brick wall. 'Buff just wanted to bang him around some for what he done to Kitty back at his uncle's house. I agreed to help out 'cause Buff wasn't big enough to handle him but when we went into Gregory's room and woke him he went nuts and I overdid it when I tried to keep him quiet. Then there wasn't nothing to do but pitch him out into the snow. I figured, the way it was coming, he wouldn't show till spring and somewhere between times I could dig him out and plant him somewheres else.'

'Who wrote the note Foote got?'

'That was Buff. He wanted to scare the old man, give him something to sweat about.'

I locked him up and went back to the hotel wondering if it was hockey, booze or too many barroom brawls that made Puck what he was and decided not to think about that too much because it might make me wonder about me.

CHAPTER TWENTY-EIGHT

When the Congregational church let out at noon I was waiting out front and pried the judge and mayor away from their wives and brought them back to the hotel parlor. They were both passive as scolded kindergartners and it took a while before I found out they had been brought to that state by the Reverend Plant's sermon. His message had been country miles away from anything expected. They went to be bullied, threatened, coaxed, forgiven and finally uplifted. Instead he talked of life's uncertainties; of human frailty, not evil; not obligations, not temptations; of failure, not damnation. It was a sermon of despair and they didn't even get to weep.

My account of what I'd learned from Buff and Puck didn't cheer them up any. The mayor sat, wagging his thick head, the judge scowled.

'You think there's anything can be done about Clint Cogswell's part in all this?' I asked the judge.

He slumped back, closed his eyes a moment, opened them and said, no, the man had done nothing actionable.

We kicked that around a little before the mayor began to revive and twitch. He finally butted in, saying his wife would be waiting dinner. The prospect cheered him enough so he stopped at the door to tell me I'd done a great job and shook my hand.

The judge shook hands with me too but the prospects of his dinner didn't distract him from what he'd heard that cold Sunday morning.

Ernie, the City Hall's janitor and chief blabbermouth, had talked with Puck while I'd been busy and by the time I got out to the lobby half of Corden knew most of the story. Ma was checking Mary Jane and her hubby out and told me Kitty had gone up to her room.

I climbed the stairs and knocked on the door to fourteen. After a moment she opened it, looked at me as if I were a stranger and said, 'What do you want?'

'You interested in what happened?'

She turned her back, walked to the bed and flopped across it.

'I know what happened. Buff froze himself to death and left me alone. The sole survivor.'

I closed the door and moved over beside her.

'Did you know he killed Arthur?'

She curled on her side, just as her brother had the night before, and covered her eyes with both hands.

'You know why he did it?' I asked.

She pulled her hands down to her chin and looked up.

'Did he tell you?'

'Yeah.'

'How'd you make him do that?'

'I woke him and wouldn't leave till he told me. It didn't take long. He wanted to unload it.'

'Uh-huh. It was nice of you to help him through that. When you were through, why didn't you put him in the cell with Puck?'

'He wanted to sleep and seemed too pooped to go anywhere. Besides, I had to talk with Puck.'

'So you turned out to be a very conscientious cop, didn't you?'

I sat on the edge of the bed and she pulled away.

'What I really wanted was to get enough dope on old Clint, the preacher's man, to nail him. He's the one behind it all.'

'Okay,' she said, turning away, 'so you wanted to do the right thing. Just don't come around here expecting me to kiss you for it.'

'You want to know why Buff killed Arthur?'

'I don't want to know another damned thing, Officer Wilcox. You got your man, or men, so now the rest of us can go, right?'

'Aren't you going to stay for Buff's funeral?'

She slipped off the bed, stood up and walked to the window.

'No, because it's not going to be here. I'm the sole survivor, I get to take him where I want and I want him out of here and John'll take care of everything so I can.'

She said that to gall me but it didn't much. I told her she could leave with her friends whenever she was ready. She said thanks and I left.

Clint was sitting in a rocker when I entered the lobby. His face, which I'd thought was craggy when we met, now looked gaunt and he had the eyes of a drunk who'd spent the night with the snakes.

Our eyes met for a second, then he looked away.

'The reverend wants to see you up in his room,' he said.

'Fine. I want to see him, and you too. Come along.'

He tried to say no but when I took his arm he came along meekly.

The Reverend Plant was posed before the window, looking down at the blanketed town under a pale sky and a cold sun. He turned as we entered, lifted his eyebrows at Clint and gave him a cold stare.

'He made me come,' Clint told him and then, after an awkward moment, walked over to his bed, sat down and slumped over with his forearms across his knees.

The reverend asked me to sit down on the straight chair by the door, moved over to his bed and settled on the edge.

'I am very happy to see your father's recovering nicely. We talked a bit ago. You know something? He's very proud of you today.'

'It won't last.'

He forced a smile. 'Perhaps not. But it's an improvement.'

'So why'd you want to see me?'

'Well,' he stirred uncomfortably, then leaned forward, 'I wanted to let you know I went over and talked with Puck when I heard what'd happened—'

'You know about Buff?'

He sat straight.

'I do. Tragic.'

'Puck told you everything?'

'He admitted killing Gregory, yes. He claims it was an accident and I believe him. I understand that will make the charge manslaughter rather than murder—'

'He tell you he and Buff also manslaughtered old Arthur?'

'He says Buff did that. Over a very old grudge.'

'Brought nice and fresh by your manager over there.'

'Puck will not substantiate any such charge. And even if he did, I doubt that it would carry much weight in court. You will get nowhere trying to drag him into this affair.'

'Or you either, right?'

He met my glare straight on.

'Who have you talked to about all of this?' he asked.

I told him.

He nodded. 'And I'm sure the judge told

you there was no case against Clint, did he not?'

I looked over at Clint. He'd stretched out on the bed and was staring at the ceiling.

'It looks like you got nothing to worry about, Reverend. Except hell, maybe. But with Clint to manage things you'll probably make out even there. They'll give you two the bridal suite.'

'We all have much to answer for,' he said. 'This trip and all of the tragedies related to it have made me realize what a total sinner I've been. God has brought me to the real truth and this is what I'll preach from now on—'

'Like you did this morning?'

'Exactly!' His eyes lit up and he got to his feet. 'You should've been there. I have never, in four decades of bringing His message, had the impact I did in that church this morning. Isn't that right, Clint?'

Clint turned toward the wall.

'The congregation left the church in total silence. I made them *think*. I made them *realize*!'

'Uh-uh. You laid an egg, preacher. You go on with that line and you'll be talking to yourself on Sundays.'

For just a second I thought I saw a glint of concern, then he shook his head and said, no, they would follow. And if they did not come in flocks, he would talk to the few and if he reached only one, he would be saved.

Their pilot picked them up late in the afternoon out at Christenson's farm. I never heard about him preaching over the radio after that or anyplace else. In fact, I never heard anything about any of them after that.

Joey got back to work in May and after helping Elihu remodel the west rooms into two more apartments, I hopped a freight and went West.

Photoset, printed and bound in Great Britain by
REDWOOD BURN LIMITED, Trowbridge, Wiltshire